Clayton Zukan is a skilled bomb maker, but he's careful to only sell his devices to those with a worthy cause, or so he thinks. He learns about shifters when an assassin disarms one of his devices and tracks him down. After his brother mates with a shifter, Clayton does his best to hide his jealousy. After all, Clayton would love a mate of his own.

The wolf shifter pack is kind enough to build Clayton a large shop with an apartment over it, so he throws himself into his work. It's pretty remote, and he likes that, so he doesn't have to watch all the mated couples' sickly sweet antics. Taking a hike, Clayton comes face to face with an animal that shouldn't be living in the mountains of Colorado — a cheetah.

When the beautiful animal transforms into an even more gorgeous man, Clayton feels the mate-pull, and he's overjoyed. Fate has brought him his very own shifter. Except, the sexy man — Bailey Dyer — claims not to know what a shifter is. When explanations begin, can Clayton convince Bailey that paranormals are not the enemy, especially after learning that Bailey volunteered for the experiment that turned him into a shifter?

An Unconventional Mating
Copyright © 2021 Charlie Richards
ISBN: 978-1-4874-3307-9
Cover art by Angela Waters

Published by eXtasy Books Inc or
Devine Destinies, an imprint of eXtasy Books Inc

Look for us online at:
www.eXtasybooks.com or www.devinedestinies.com

An Unconventional Mating
Wolves of Stone Ridge Book Fifty-Five

By

Charlie Richards

DEDICATION

*All the war-propaganda, all the screaming and lies and hatred,
comes invariably from people who are not fighting.*
~George Orwell

CHAPTER ONE

The soft beep of a machine cut through the haze permeating his mind. He twitched his fingers, intending to swing his arm and slap his alarm clock. His foggy brain insisted that he needed a bit more sleep.

Except, he couldn't lift his arm. His appendage felt heavy, oh-so-heavy . . . and weak. His muscles screamed just from the effort of wiggling his fingers.

What the hell happened to me?

Then the beeping sped up a smidge, and he realized he had to be in the hospital.

Heart monitor, but why?

Forcing himself to slow his breathing, he heard the beeping slow back down again, too.

Okay. Think. What happened?

Nothing came to mind.

Then what's the last thing I do remember?

His mind remained stubbornly blank.

Shit.

Then something else occurred to him . . . or *didn't* occur to him.

Uh, what's my name?

Once more, his mind remained stubbornly blank.

The heart monitor began beeping faster again.

He swallowed hard and returned his focus to his breathing. Unfortunately, he couldn't keep his thoughts from racing. His brain screamed that something was wrong—*so very wrong!*

"Hey, hey, easy there."

A soft melodic tenor cut through his rising panic. He felt hands land on his arms, pushing him back on the bed, although he wasn't certain when he'd begun struggling to rise.

"Just relax, Bailey," the man urged, continuing to press him to the bed. "Just sleep a while longer. Then everything will make sense."

Bailey.

He latched onto that. His name was Bailey. Before he could ask for more information, like what the hell was going on, whatever sedative the man gave him took effect, and he slipped back into sleep.

When Bailey drifted to wakefulness, he remained perfectly still and listened. The beeping continued, but he didn't hear any other sounds. With the way his breathing sounded so loud in his ears, he worried he would miss any other noises.

Bailey heard soft footsteps on floorboards, the noises coming from below him. Realizing there was someone in the building, he hoped there wasn't anyone in the room, too, as he worked his eyelids open. It took an excessive number of blinks, but he finally managed to focus on his surroundings.

Confusion flooded him. He wasn't in a hospital room. While there was obvious medical equipment here and there, the medium tan walls, forest pictures upon them, and the green duvet covering him screamed a private home.

A private medical facility, maybe?

A vision of sterile white walls flashed before his mind. He frowned, uncertainty filling him anew. While he remembered his name — Bailey — due to whoever was caring for him —

Wait, what if they're not caring for me? What if they're holding me hostage? Is that why that guy put me back to sleep?

Some inner voice Bailey didn't recognize screamed that they needed to escape. They needed to find shelter and safety while he sorted out his memories. His need to flee, while unfamiliar, began to dominate his thoughts.

Spotting the IV in his left arm, Bailey reached for it. He paused before making contact, hesitating. Peering up the line, he tried to read the label, but it was just a string of characters that didn't make sense to him.

Unwilling to trust whatever the strange liquid was, Bailey eased the IV from his arm. He grimaced and tossed the needle to the floor, then pressed a corner of the sheet to the mark. His arm stung for a few seconds, but the pain swiftly eased.

Bailey lifted the blanket, surprised to see the wound was already closed, new pink flesh covering it. Shaking his head, he pulled the clip off of his finger. The machine monitoring his pulse immediately began to beep loudly.

Hissing, Bailey shoved from the bed. His legs nearly buckled, and his head swam at the movement. Only grabbing the nightstand and dresser kept him on his feet. After a few seconds, he managed to reach over and yank the machine's plug from the wall.

The blessed silence that followed concerned Bailey almost as much as the noise had. He focused on listening for footsteps below as he took one slow breath after another. Upon hearing the quiet murmur of voices, then the soft thud of footfalls, he knew he needed to hurry.

Still using the nightstand as support, Bailey eased past the machine to the window behind it. He pushed up, fully expecting it not to budge. When it slid up easily, he nearly tumbled out of it.

Bailey caught himself on the sill and stared. Directly below him was an expansive back deck. A huge built-in grill stood off to the left on a stone patio. Beyond that was an even larger spread of green lawn that backed up to pines . . . pines as far as Bailey's eyes could see.

A desire to run, to climb and jump, flooded him. He frowned, uncertain from where it stemmed. Even as a kid, he hadn't been a climber.

Wait. Or was I?

The sense memory remained just out of reach.

Frustration mixed with fear.

Why can't I remember anything?

The creak of footsteps on the stairs reached Bailey. He returned his focus to the far trees. Glancing down, he wondered if he had enough strength to climb down the drain pipe at the corner of the house.

Bailey heard a voice from outside his room, one he recognized from before, say, "That's odd. The beeping stopped."

Someone answered, "Crapballs. That can't be good."

His decision made, Bailey knew he had to chance it. He swung his leg over the windowsill. Balancing carefully while gripping the window frame, Bailey swung his leg and hooked his heel around the side of the downspout. Then he reached up and grabbed the rain gutter.

As soon as Bailey swung out, placing all his weight on the aluminum, it tore from the building, and he fell.

Bailey's cry of shock almost drowned out a man yelling, "Wait! Bailey, stop!"

To Bailey's surprise, he landed on all fours — a little dizzy, but unharmed.

"Oh, damn," the second male stated.

Looking up, Bailey spotted two men peering down at him. One was a slender blond, and the second was a black male. Even from the ground, he could tell that both would fall into the category of twinks.

I could have taken them easily.

"I guess now we know what kind of animal he is," the black man commented.

As the blond nodded, he called down, "Please give us a chance to explain, Bailey. At least, don't go anywhere until your brother gets here."

Bailey didn't know what the guy was talking about, and he didn't plan on sticking around to find out. Turning, he bounded toward the trees. As soon as he could, he leaped onto one, digging in his claws.

Even as Bailey wondered where they came from and how he could move like this, it felt as natural as breathing. He galloped along a pine branch, leaving the strangers behind him. Even in the distance, he still managed to hear the blond's voice.

"Oh, damn. Declan's not going to like this."

Bounding from branch to branch, Bailey relished the freedom after waking in that small room. He fatigued quickly, though, making him wonder how long he'd been lying in that bed. Pausing, he sat on a branch and peered around.

Bailey didn't recognize anything. As far as he could see, there were pine branches. Below him, there was the forest floor of needles, dirt, and rocks. He wasn't entirely confident from which direction he'd come, either.

Twitching his tail idly, Bailey wondered what he should do and where he should go. He figured his best bet was to stay in cat form, allowing him to run and climb faster and farther than as a naked human.

Is that an odd thought?

Bailey wasn't certain . . . again.

Sighing, Bailey sprawled on the branch and took a few minutes to catch his breath. He also took the time to decide what to do. Not knowing the area, he didn't want to chance running into a town. People there could be in league with those who'd been holding him.

Deciding heading up the mountain was his best bet, Bailey heaved back to his feet and began moving. He padded slowly from branch to branch, taking his time to pay attention to his surroundings. Bailey wanted to remember his path from then on.

As Bailey wandered forward, he felt his stomach rumble. He lifted his nose to the air and inhaled deeply. A myriad of scents teased his senses, but one stood out to him.

Prey.

Bailey paused and sniffed again, licking his lips in anticipation. Deciding the direction the other animal was in, he began creeping toward it. With the way the wind blew, he knew he was downwind, allowing him to get quite close.

Peering through the pine boughs, Bailey spotted a large squirrel sitting on a lower branch. He crouched, preparing, then leaped. Dropping the ten feet, he landed with his back paws on the branch and his front ones on the unsuspecting critter. A swift bite to its body snapped its neck before it could even squeal in alarm.

Flipping over the squirrel, Bailey bit into the animal's belly, tearing it open. He chomped on the meat, ignoring the fur as the blood oozed around his teeth. Swallowing the flesh and blood, he rumbled happily.

Bailey ate almost all of it, even most of the bones. When he was done, only a bit of fur and the empty skull remained. He'd even sucked out the brains and eyeballs, enjoying the tasty, succulent flesh.

Licking his lips, Bailey cleaned his whiskers. Then he lifted each front paw and cleaned his claws and toes. He followed that up by licking down his sides and using a damp paw to wash his face and neck.

Once Bailey finished that, he sat quietly on the branch and listened to his surroundings. After several minutes, the natural noises of the woods resumed—birds tweeted, animals chittered, and insects buzzed. Bailey felt somewhat satisfied, although, he vowed to keep a sharp eye and nose on the lookout for something larger and more filling.

Rising to his feet, Bailey started on his way again. He jogged along tree branches, jumping from one to another. Reveling in the freedom, he bounded along, taking in everything around him.

Finally, Bailey came to a cliff face. Craggy rocks rose above him. Halfway up, he spotted the edge of a dark opening.

A cave.

Bailey figured that would be the perfect place to hide out and think, giving him time to remember what had happened to him. Although his cat wasn't designed for rock climbing, he still found a way. He carefully leaped from one ledge to another until he reached his destination.

Once there, Bailey saw a small ledge in front of the cave opening almost six feet wide. The cave opening itself was quite a bit larger than he'd anticipated, perhaps five feet tall and three feet at the widest. There was also a narrow trail along the rock face leading downward.

Even as Bailey wondered where it came out on the other end, he turned his attention to the cave. He padded inside, his sharp feline eyes easily piercing the darkness, and he took in the interior.

The cave wasn't a big space — maybe twenty-five feet in an oblong pattern — but Bailey didn't need much. There was a ledge five feet off the ground deep to the left that would be comfortable for lounging. It also allowed him to watch the opening, just in case.

Inside it was cooler than outside, causing a shiver to go through Bailey's body. He knew he would get used to it, though. His cat's fur would keep him warm as soon as he acclimated to the climate.

Hope that doesn't take too long.

Bailey jumped onto the ledge and circled a couple of times. Then, finding the position he wanted, he lay down. He curled his tail around his body in an effort to keep in the heat and rested his head on his paws.

Within minutes, the day caught up with him, and sleep tugged him under.

A soft scuff-scuff with the occasional crackle of falling rocks pulled Bailey from his sleep. He remained still as he strained his ears. After a few seconds, he registered the sound of humming.

Someone was coming.

Bailey bit back a growl of frustration. All he wanted was to be left alone. How could he have such bad luck as to be immediately stumbled upon by someone?

Perhaps they won't come in here.

Keeping still, Bailey continued to listen. For some reason, the soft tones of whoever was humming sounded very pleasing to his ears. It warmed him from the inside out, and he wanted to rest his head on the person's chest and feel the vibration within his own body.

Confused by the response, tension filled him.

Just another thing I don't understand.

Then a shadow fell across the doorway.

As Bailey watched, a slender form appeared inside the doorway. He straightened from where he'd dipped just a bit to enter. His frame was clearly masculine as he pulled off a backpack, allowing it to hang on his elbow.

The man pulled a flashlight from his bag and snapped it on before placing the bag on the ground. Then he swept his beam around the cave. He continued humming as he headed to the right, away from Bailey's perch, and the light from outside illuminated the man's features.

The guy stood maybe five-foot-seven, and his bulky sweatshirt and jeans did nothing to hide his slender frame. His blond hair gleamed in the afternoon light and was held back by a bandana. Bailey felt an odd urge to remove the cloth so he could see how long the man's hair was.

Would it feel silky between my fingers?

Another thing that reached Bailey was the man's scent—earthy, masculine goodness with just a hint of burnt metal, which he didn't understand. Still, it culminated in a delicious aroma that he wanted to smell more of. He wondered if the man's kiss would taste just as good.

A rumble of desire escaped Bailey.

The noise drew the human's attention.

The guy swung around, and his light illuminated Bailey. Gasping, he backed up a step, which pressed his back to the wall.

"Oh, wow," the man mumbled. His wide blue eyes peered at Bailey. "I-I'm sorry, kitty." He began sliding toward the exit. "Just stay there, pretty cat," he murmured softly. "I'll leave you alone. Last time I was here, there wasn't any sign of anything living in here." The man took another step toward the exit, repeating, "I'll just leave you alone."

It hit Bailey that the human was leaving, and he didn't want that—not at all. Rising to his feet, he growled in warning. To his pleasure, the man froze.

Except Bailey really hated the stench of fear that began permeating the cave.

"I'm going to die," the man whimpered. "Oh, gods. Please don't eat me."

Bailey realized he *did* want to eat the man . . . just not in the way the guy was afraid of. Knowing he needed to be able to speak, he began to shift.

CHAPTER TWO

I'm too young to die!
Fear permeated every cell of Clayton Zukan's body. Never in his wildest dreams would he have guessed he would end up as cat chowder.

And what a cat it is.

"What the hell is a cheetah doing in the mountains?" Clayton had always rambled and talked to himself, especially when he was nervous. "You're not supposed to be here."

To Clayton's surprise, he spotted a tell-tale rippling of skin. That was followed by twitching limbs and the crack and pop of adjusting bones and ligaments. The fur disappeared to be replaced by human skin—lots and lots of lightly bronzed and sexy naked skin.

"Oh damn," Clayton whispered, unable to help but stare at the stranger. "You're a shifter."

The man cocked his head as he swung his legs off the side of the rock ledge. "A shifter?" As he eased off the side with a wince, his half-hard cock and large balls were on clear display. "I'm Bailey . . . I think." Stalking toward Clayton, he added, "I didn't mean to scare you. I didn't want you to go."

Tongue-tied, his attention on the naked man's gorgeous frame, Clayton stared. The man had dark hair, either dark-brown or black, that reached his ears. His dark eyes glittered in the dim lighting. His body was all lean muscle and toned limbs, and Clayton's fingers twitched to touch.

Except, Clayton knew better than to touch a shifter without permission. While he was a human, he lived near the beta of the local wolf pack. To a shifter, nudity was perfectly natural, since they had to get naked to shift or get stuck in clothes.

"Hey," the man—Bailey—crooned. "What's your name, cutie?"

Then Bailey reached out and cradled Clayton's jaw, teasing his thumb under his bottom lip. "I-I'm Clayton. Um, Clayton Zukan."

"So very nice to meet you, cute Clay," Bailey rumbled, resting his second hand on his shoulder. He sidled even closer as he swept his gaze over him. "Please tell me you're gay. Or at least bi." His smile turned predatory as he added, "Because you smell so fucking good, and I wanna fuck you in the worst way."

"I-I'm gay," Clayton replied, uncertain if he actually liked being called cute Clay, but something else seemed more important. "I smell good to you?"

Considering Clayton had spent the last two days focused on making a cool new explosive device, then had immediately decided to decompress by going for a hike and picnic, he couldn't figure out why anyone would think he smelled good. He hadn't even taken the time to shower before gathering what he needed and heading into the woods. In the past, he'd always cleared his head by enjoying a sauna in the hidden, underground bunkers he and his brother, Castrose, had lived in. That had been before one of his bombs had been purchased by a lying shifter, who had exposed Clayton to the paranormal world.

Clayton could hardly wait to show Alpha Declan and Prier Bozeman the new bomb he'd just finished. They could use it to continue liberating paranormals from government facilities. It would also just be fun to blow something up.

Clayton knew that Prier would get a kick out of that, even if Declan wouldn't.

Except, Clayton had needed time to decompress first, so

he'd gone to enjoy nature.

"Yes, you smell fantastic." Then Bailey tucked his nose against Clayton's neck and inhaled deeply. On a groan, he muttered, "So fucking good."

Even as arousal surged through Clayton, excitement of a different sort filled him. "D-Do y-you think" — he tipped his head to the side, offering Bailey more room to snuffle, lick, and nip his skin — "mmm, that I could be your mate?"

Clayton had wanted his own shifter mate since he'd learned what it meant. He'd met every single shifter in Alpha Declan's pack, even the women. Unfortunately, none of them had been a match.

Chuckling roughly, Bailey muttered, "If mating means fucking, hell yeah." Then he slid the hand on his jaw around to cup his nape. "Gonna kiss you."

Bailey didn't wait for permission. Instead, he just took. He dipped his head while tightening his hand on Clayton's nape, holding him steady, and sealed his mouth over Clayton's own.

Clayton felt Bailey nip his bottom lip, and he opened on instinct. His mouth was instantly filled with the rich masculine flavor of the other man. He welcomed his soon-to-be lover's appendage, dueling it with his own as he grabbed the guy's shoulders and clung, reveling in the feel of the smooth, hard flesh beneath his palms.

Sliding his hand from Clayton's shoulder down to wrap around his waist, Bailey pulled him tight against his body. He eased his fingers under Clayton's sweatshirt, teasing up his spine. At the same time, Bailey used his hold on his neck to ravish his mouth.

Reveling in Bailey's aggressive hunger, Clayton went with the flow. His tongue teased against Bailey's, and he curled his fingers into the man's flesh. He felt tingles erupt over the flesh of his back to trickle around his torso until his nipples beaded.

Finally, only because the need to breathe intruded, Clayton turned his head and broke the kiss on a gasp.

Bailey growled softly as he began nuzzling Clayton's temple. "You taste delicious, too." Licking at his skin, he added, "Can't wait to taste you everywhere."

Clayton snickered as he heard those words. "Honestly, can't see how I taste so great," he admitted with a grimace. "I've been working for several days and didn't take the time to brush my teeth or shower before leaving on my hike."

Humming, Bailey murmured, "I'm not certain when I last brushed my teeth." His chuckle sounded husky as he added, "Maybe we both taste terrible, and we just can't tell."

Snorting, Clayton turned his head to the side, offering more of his neck to Bailey. "Then maybe we should never brush our teeth again, 'cause I sure like how you taste."

Bailey's snickers were cut off when he began sucking on Clayton's neck tendon.

Clayton's mind began to shut down as heat and lust flowed through him. Except . . . wait. "Why can't you remember?"

"Talk later, Clay," Bailey replied, sliding his hands to both of Clayton's ass cheeks. "Fuck now."

The possessive hold yanked a groan of pleasure from Clayton's throat. "Okay."

Bailey wasted no time in gripping the hem of his sweatshirt and pulling it over his head. He followed up by popping the button on his jeans and undoing his fly. Then he dropped to his knees and tugged them down, underwear and all.

Clayton swung his arms, losing his balance upon feeling the swift moves on his body.

Immediately, Bailey noticed his predicament. He grabbed his waist and steadied him. Peering up at him, he winked before pressing his nose against Clayton's groin. Nuzzling softly, Bailey inhaled noisily.

Then Bailey let that breath out in a low groan. "Soooo,

good."

Before Clayton could even think of coming up with a response, Bailey swallowed his dick to the root.

Barking in shock—and pleasure—Clayton shuddered hard. His cock flexed in the delicious hot pressure of Bailey's wet mouth. He grabbed the kneeling shifter's shoulders as the man sucked up, practically causing his balls to pull up with it.

"B-Bailey," Clayton whined, unable to help himself. "Gonna—"

"Do it," Bailey demanded, pulling off his prick for only long enough to bark the words. Then he went back to sucking Clayton's cock.

Clayton knew he would feel embarrassed later, but he couldn't control himself. His balls tightened, and tingles erupted down his spine. He whined in pleasure as his orgasm crashed through his system.

Bliss surged through him, and he swayed. His eyes threatened to roll to the back of his head, and he blinked swiftly to clear the spots dancing across his vision. When he gathered himself again, he realized Bailey still suckled on his cock head even as he had a finger in his ass and was stretching him.

Before Clayton could process the sting, Bailey teased his prostate. A zing of pleasure coursed through his groin. His dick, still in his new lover's mouth, twitched, remaining hard as nails.

"Bailey," Clayton whined, too over-sensitized to feel shame. "Too much."

"Relax, Clay," Bailey crooned, popping off his cock. "I got you."

Then Bailey eased his fingers from Clayton's chute—*when did he add a second one*—and urged him to turn around.

"On your knees, cutie," Bailey urged. "Need in you."

As Clayton began to obey, his scrambled thoughts cleared

a little. "Uh, wait," he cried. "Wait."

Bailey whined his name before saying, "Clay, what?"

"Blanket and lube," Clayton gasped out. "More comfortable on my boney knees."

Even as Bailey growled softly, he eased his grip on Clayton. "Get it and hurry," he urged. "Can't wait much longer."

A quick glance at Bailey's prick told Clayton exactly what his lover meant. He also gulped at the sight of the deep-red, painful-looking erection jutting from the man's groin. The wide, flared head leaked pre-cum so copiously that the translucent fluid was dripping from his crown.

The expression of discomfort on Bailey's face also spurred him into action.

Clayton swiftly grabbed his backpack. He yanked open the zipper and pulled out the blanket. His movements jerky and urgent, he spread it out—mostly. As Clayton awkwardly kicked off his sandals, pants, and underwear, he grabbed the lube from the front pocket of the bag.

On his knees and one hand, Clayton used the other to wave the tube, holding it over his shoulder. "Hurry, Bailey," he urged. "Take me."

Bailey growled as he snagged the lube from him. "Not that I'm not grateful, but why do you have lube?" he asked gruffly, jealousy filling his tone. "Were you meeting someone?"

As Bailey spoke, he rested one hand on Clayton's hip. Teasing his fingertips along Clayton's hip bone caused the skin of his hip to goose bump. It also caused his still mostly-hard prick to thicken anew, distracting him.

"Tell me," Bailey demanded, drizzling a dollop of slick directly onto Clayton's hole. "Who is it? He's never to touch you again."

Clayton felt his cheeks heat for a new reason, but he forced the words out of him. "I wasn't meeting anyone," he admitted. "I was gonna jack off before eating."

Bailey groaned softly while inserting first one finger, then a second, into Clayton's channel. "God, I'd love to see that," he rumbled. "So fucking hot."

Panting softly, Clayton forced his body to relax and accept the intrusion, which had quickly become three fingers. "M-Maybe s-someday."

"Definitely someday," Bailey countered as he pulled his fingers free. A second later, he pressed the head of his cock against Clayton's opening. "Push out."

Obeying, Clayton breathed out. He felt his guardian muscle stretch, his body accepting Bailey's thick crown. The heat of the shifter's erection sank deep into his body as he pushed into him with one long, smooth thrust.

Once Bailey pressed his groin flush to Clayton's ass, his balls nestled against Clayton's own, he sighed deeply and stopped. He draped his body over Clayton's and nuzzled his neck. Licking and nipping along his flesh, Bailey hummed while skimming his right hand over Clayton's chest—his weight supported on his left—teasing at his nipples.

"You feel so good," Bailey growled, drawing out his words as he slowly began withdrawing. "So good." Reversing direction, he eased back into him. "Don't remember anything feeling so good."

Clayton moaned and arched beneath him, urging Bailey with his body. The muscles in his chute flared to life upon feeling his lover's erection slide within him. His shifter's fingers plucking his nipples sent pulses of pleasure through his torso. When Bailey hit his prostate, Clayton cried his lover's name as his cock throbbed.

"Yessss," Bailey hissed, speeding up his movements while hitting Clayton's prostate with each thrust. "Call my name," he demanded. "Cry out who's giving you such pleasure."

Clayton's mind began to haze as ecstasy flooded his body. The movement of Bailey's hips sent delicious zings through his rectum and out to his groin. His shifter's hand continued to work his sensitive nipples, creating heady waves of heat over Clayton's body.

"Come for me," Bailey demanded roughly in his ear. "Squeeze my cock. Milk my seed from me."

As Bailey issued his throaty demands, he moved his hand to Clayton's aching shaft. He began jacking him in time with his thrusts. On one down stroke, Bailey teased his fingertips over the sensitive flesh of Clayton's ball sack.

That was the final straw.

"Bailey!" Clayton screamed as his testicles tightened, pumping his cum from him.

Groaning roughly, Bailey buried his prick deep in Clayton's body as a shudder passed through him. He pressed his face against Clayton's neck. As another shudder took the shifter draped over him, Clayton felt the teeth at his neck.

Tipping his head a little, Clayton welcomed the action. With his senses soaring from the greatest double-orgasm of his life, he could think of no reason to deny Bailey's claim. As a shifter, they would twine their lives together and figure out all the rest later.

Clayton knew that was how shifters worked.

A low growl sounded from the man behind him right before Bailey sank his teeth into Clayton's flesh.

Opening his mouth on a pain-filled gasp, for an instant, Clayton thought the tales of the pleasure of claiming bites was a lie. Then, as Bailey began sucking on his neck, the most exquisite tendrils of sensation spread through his system. His nipples beaded, and his cock thickened.

Clayton moaned as a third orgasm swamped his senses. His eyes rolled to the back of his head, and a hard jolt of ecstasy coursed through him. He moaned Bailey's name as his arms gave out. If it weren't for Bailey's grip, he would have landed on his face.

Breathing raggedly, Clayton trembled while the hairs on his arms stood on end.

The feel of Bailey easing his teeth from his neck sent a fresh wash of tingles through his torso. His tongue licking at his neck made his nipples bead. Even how he pressed a kiss to where he'd bitten him caused a zing to shoot through him.

"Wow," Clayton slurred. "So that's what it feels like."

"What's that?" Bailey murmured against his neck.

"A claiming bite," Clayton answered absently.

Bailey eased them to their sides on the blanket, still keeping his prick firmly embedded in him. "What's that mean?" he asked as he rubbed over Clayton's chest, mapping his lean lines.

Clayton opened his mouth, then snapped it shut again. Frowning, he stared at the stone wall five feet away. His mind whirled with the meaning of that question.

Swallowing hard, Clayton softly asked, "You're a shifter, and you don't know what a claiming bite means?"

"No. Sorry." Bailey continued to nuzzle his nape. "Is it important?"

Tensing, Clayton felt his heartrate ratchet up for a new reason. "Um . . . yeah. Very," he whispered. Clamping his hand onto Bailey's wrist, he added, "You, uh, you essentially married us."

Bailey finally pulled his prick free only to push Clayton onto his back. He stared down at him, lines of shock clear on his face.

"Married us?"

Clayton sighed deeply as he recalled Bailey telling him he couldn't remember . . . much of anything. "Oh, shit."

CHAPTER THREE

M*arried? What the fuck?*
"Are you serious?" Bailey asked again, not believing it the first time.

"Yes."

Clayton's voice was soft and uncertain. Bailey could feel the tension in the body sprawled beneath his own. Even as his mind reeled with that revelation, he felt the strangest desire to soothe his clearly upset lover.

Resting his weight on his left forearm, Bailey skimmed his right hand up Clayton's torso, rubbing soothingly. His lover, while the most gorgeous man he'd ever seen, really was a little on the thin side. A need to feed the man, to take care of him, surged through him, confusing him even more. After all, they'd just met, and they didn't know anything about each other.

I don't know anything about me, either.

And that's another issue.

Pushing that problem aside for another time, Bailey commented slowly, "You knew that a bite from a, a shifter would marry you and me."

Upon seeing Clayton's Adam's apple bob as he swallowed hard, Bailey barely resisted the urge to lick the nub.

Damn. What is it about this guy?

"Yes," Clayton whispered again.

Snapping his focus back to Clayton's eyes, Bailey saw the wariness there, the uncertainty. "Then why let me?" He didn't understand.

Clayton sighed, and he cut his focus to the left.

Hell, no.

Bailey threaded his fingers through Clayton's slightly shaggy, pale-blond hair and used the hold to get him to return his regard. "Why?"

Peering into Clayton's light-blue eyes, Bailey saw something unexpected — longing. Even as shocking as the turn of events was, he couldn't find it in himself to be upset. He was just so damn confused.

"Talk to me," Bailey urged, massaging Clayton's scalp. He slung his right leg over his lover's thighs, cuddling close. Bending his elbow, he rested his hand in his palm so he could continue staring at the man in a more relaxed way. "You seem to know something about what's going on between us. Share with me."

For several heartbeats, Clayton nibbled his plump lower lip. He swept his gaze over Bailey's face, searching for . . . something.

Bailey waited patiently, doing his best to soothe the nervous man with a scalp massage.

Clayton sighed deeply, then admitted, "I've been living with your kind for months, and I've always wanted the sort of bonds I see between mated shifters." His eyes seemed to gleam in the dim cave lighting, but still, Bailey spotted the hopefulness within their depths. "Meeting you, experiencing the attraction, hearing how much you needed me and enjoyed my scent . . . all the signs were there. I'm your mate, and you're my shifter." Curving his lips in a tremulous smile, Clayton whispered, "I didn't want to resist you. I want what we could build together."

Build together.

His lover sounded so damn hopeful.

Knowing only truth would do, Bailey told him, "This morning, I woke up in the bed of a private clinic with needles in me. The people there called me Bailey, but I don't know if that's really my name." He continued to hold Clayton's gaze, taking in the concern that replaced his hope. "Something happened to me, and I don't know what. I have no memory of my time before today."

Clayton's eyes widened, and he gripped Bailey's upper arms. "There are people capturing and experimenting on shifters," he told him, a mixture of excitement and concern in his tone. "I bet that's what happened to you. I have friends that can help."

Bailey weighed the pros and cons. On the one hand, he could really use help to understand what had happened to him. On the other, he didn't know who he could trust.

Can I trust Clayton?

Realizing there really was no decision to make, not unless Bailey wanted to spend the rest of his days hiding in a cave, he nodded slowly. "Don't tell too many people about me, yet, please," he ordered, uncertain if he was doing the right thing. "And only contact someone you trust."

Clayton smiled at him. "I'll call my brother. He's mated with a shifter, too," he stated. "He'll come here if I ask, and we can go from there. Okay?"

After licking his lips once, Bailey forced a tight smile. "Sure. Okay."

When Clayton began to roll to the side and reach for his bag, Bailey tightened his hold for an instant. He saw the questioning look on his lover's face and loosened his grip a little. Still, he only gave him enough space to grab his bag and pull it toward them.

The smile on Clayton's face made Bailey think that his lover actually liked the treatment.

Huh.

Clayton relaxed back on their make-shift bed. Smiling up at him, he dialed a number on his phone. Then he lifted it to his ear.

Bailey eased onto the blanket beside him, resting his head

on his arm and sliding it under Clayton so he could do the same. Wrapping his other arm around his lover's torso, he cuddled him close. He glanced between the scar he'd left on Clayton's shoulder, feeling a measure of satisfaction he couldn't begin to understand, and the man's face, taking in his clear happiness.

When the ringing Bailey heard ended, a deep voice greeted, "Hey, Clay. You finish with your new bomb?"

Lifting his brows, Bailey mouthed, *Bomb?*

Clayton laughed. "I did, and it's awesome, but that's not why I'm calling."

"Really?" the man replied, sounding surprised. "Then what's up?"

"I found my mate!" Clayton cried, a huge grin spreading across his face. When there were several heartbeats of silence through the line, Clayton pulled the phone away and looked at the screen, obviously checking the connection. After confirming they were still on a call together, Clayton returned the phone to his ear and asked, "Cass? Castrose? Did you hear me?"

"Your mate?" Castrose sounded wary and concerned. "Where? When? Where are you, Clay?"

"Yeah, in the mountains. Do you remember that cave you and I found last month?" Clayton still smiled as he relayed their position to Castrose. "The one on the south cliff side?"

"I do." Castrose quickly continued, "You met a shifter in those woods? Or is he something other?"

Other?

"Yeah, Bailey's a shifter," Clayton confirmed. Then, holding his gaze, he added, "But he escaped from somewhere, and he's understandably wary. Will just you and Eion come for now?"

After a few heartbeats, Castrose replied, "Yes. We'll be there in less than an hour. Don't move."

Without waiting for a reply, Castrose disconnected the call.

Clayton evidently didn't find that odd. Placing the phone aside, he smiled at Bailey. "That'll give us time to eat and chat and stuff."

"And stuff?" Bailey didn't know what *and stuff* was, but from the way his prick twitched, he could think of a way or two for them to fill the time.

Then his stomach rumbled.

Chuckling, Clayton winked. "I saw that look. You can have my ass again after we eat."

Groaning, Bailey nodded, doing his best to push aside his desires. He rolled off of Clayton, immediately missing the warmth of his body. Rocking to a sitting position, he crossed his legs Indian-style and watched his lover grab his backpack once more.

Clayton pulled out a thermos and set it on the nearby stone. "That's this amazing Thai curry-flavored beef bone broth that I absolutely love. Amazing source of protein." When he revealed a long, slender plastic container, he claimed, "Deviled eggs made with olive oil mayo, so awesome source of protein and fat." Finally, Clayton lifted a bag of radishes and carrots as well as a bottle of ranch dressing. "And for our carbs, tasty veggies."

It wasn't until Clayton glanced his way and winked, saying, "I'm not going anywhere, Bailey," that Bailey realized he'd been watching the man's every move as if ready to grab him if he got too far away.

Huh. Guess there's definitely something to this being mates thing.

Shaking his head, Bailey forced a rueful smile as he rubbed the back of his neck. "Sorry. Not used to . . . any of this, I guess." Focusing on the food, he mused, "You seem very health-conscious, but you're so slender." Concern rode him as he asked, "Are you ill?"

Clayton's skin pinked a little as he shook his head. "Oh, no. My brother, Castrose, stocks my fridge. I don't cook, like, at all." As he poured some of the bone broth into the lid of the thermos, he told him, "I can wire the most intricate of bombs, but put me in front of a stove, and I'll burn the house down."

"You mentioned bombs before." Bailey took the fragrant broth his lover handed to him. "How'd you, uh, get into that?" Then he took a tentative sip of the brew. When the fluid flowed over his taste buds, he hummed appreciatively and swallowed a much larger mouthful. "Oh, that's good."

Grinning, Clayton nodded. "Told ya." He opened the container next, revealing the paprika-sprinkled deviled eggs. "Try these. My brother's mate, Eion, makes them. They're amazing, too."

As Bailey picked one up, he eyed it speculatively as he murmured, "It's odd. I remember that this red powder is paprika, and when you said deviled eggs, I knew what to expect." Shaking his head, he grumbled, "How come I can't remember what happened to me?"

Then Bailey popped the whole thing into his mouth. He groaned in enjoyment, closing his eyes for a few seconds as he chewed. His stomach grumbled again, telling him that the squirrel hadn't been nearly enough.

Bailey opened his eyes again when Clayton asked, "What do you remember?"

After swallowing, Bailey told him, "Basic stuff. How to catch small game. How to shift." He pointed at the food. "When you talked about protein and fat and carbs, I understood what you meant." Picking up another deviled egg, Bailey eyed the slender man sitting naked next to him. "I know what bombs are." Then he gobbled the delicious food.

"But you don't remember your identity," Clayton murmured, a contemplative expression on his face. "I wonder if they could have been pumping you with something that took away certain memories, like your identity, but then kept most everything else. Motor functions and general information."

"There's people that can do that?" Bailey frowned even as he took another sip of bone broth before handing the lid to Clayton. "God, that's just insane." Cocking his head, he focused on Clayton, watching the other man also take a long sip of the bone broth. After he'd swallowed the drink, Bailey asked, "So, how do you know about all this?"

"About all what?" Clayton didn't seem to be trying to deflect as he dipped a carrot stick into some ranch dressing and popped the veggie into his mouth.

Grabbing a radish for himself, Bailey skipped the dressing as he elaborated. "Well, you call my kind shifters but say you're human. Is it common for humans to know about shifters?" He wasn't certain why, but that didn't feel right. For some reason, it also bothered him to be called one, even though the odd presence in his mind rumbled in approval. "And experiments. Where did you find out about those? And how did you learn to make bombs?" Bailey eyed his lover speculatively. "No offense, because I love how you look, but you don't look like military at all."

"That's because he's not military," came a deep voice from the entrance of the cave. As he continued speaking, a tall, thickly muscled blond stepped into view. "*I* am."

Tension tightened every muscle in Bailey's body—not from the sheer size of the stranger, but due to the pistol he had strapped to his thigh. Warily, he climbed to his feet, wondering how the hell he'd missed the man's approach.

"Cass," Clayton cried, sounding way too happy for Bailey's tastes. "Damn, you got here fast." Then his eyes widened, and he made a grab for his pants. "Crap." Clayton tossed his sweatshirt at Bailey, ordering, "Cover up. My brother shouldn't see my man's junk."

Even knowing the guy was Clayton's brother, Bailey still eyed him warily. He caught the shirt on instinct and did as his lover ordered.

Once Clayton had his pants in place—*too bad*—he stepped toward Castrose, his hand extended as if to touch him.

Bailey gripped Clayton's upper arm and tugged him to his side. Releasing his hold, he quickly wrapped the arm around his waist instead.

Clayton cast an amused glance up at him, but he didn't attempt to get away. Turning a grin on his brother, he stated, "This is Bailey, and he's my mate." With a pleased-looking smile, he added, "We just mated, so it's understandable that he wants me close. Right?"

"That *is* the way of the shifter." A second man entered the cave—a black-haired, tanned-skinned male who smelled like wolf.

How the hell do I know that?

"But he's *not* a shifter," the stranger claimed. "Not really."

While a fresh wave of confusion filled Bailey, Clayton countered, "But I saw him change, Eion. When I walked in here, he was in cheetah form." Scoffing, he added, "Good thing he was a shifter, too, because otherwise, I would have been kitty chow."

Castrose growled softly, glaring at Clayton. "You walked into a cave without your gun drawn? How could you be so careless?"

Clayton frowned petulantly at the huge man. "Well, we'd been here together just a couple of weeks ago, and there was no sign of animal habitation." His fingers tightened against Bailey's back where he had his arm around him. "You said so yourself."

Eion rested his hand on Castrose's back and rubbed up and down. "Relax, my mate," he crooned. "Your brother is fine. Our missing person is found, and everything will be well."

Waving his hand back and forth, indicating how Bailey held Clayton, Castrose grumbled, "Except, he's not really a shifter. Why the hell do they think they're mates?"

"Miach had enough shifter genes pumped into him to mate

him with Nick," Eion countered, mentioning people Bailey had never heard of. "Why not him, too?" Then he pointed. "Besides, the scent of sex is heavy in here, and your brother has a bite mark on his neck."

"Fuck," Castrose grumbled, scowling.

Bailey had had enough. "What's going on here?" he demanded. "Why do you keep saying I'm not a shifter when clearly I am?"

Castrose growled under his breath as he pinned a cool look on him. "Your name is Bailey Dyer. You were in the military. Somehow, you ended up in a covert military hospital being experimented on," he told him bluntly. "Your brother, Ronan, secreted you out. You were in a coma for over eight months until your brother met a wolf shifter, and our people stepped in to help." Narrowing his eyes, Castrose asked, "Any idea how you ended up in a military hospital being given shifter DNA?"

Upon hearing that news, memories rushed through Bailey's brain—fast and furious. Images and voices blurred, but one thing stood out to him.

I volunteered.

Then darkness took him.

CHAPTER FOUR

Clayton felt Bailey sway, but he was still unprepared for him to drop. Wrapping his arms around his waist, he held on for all he was worth. Still, if it hadn't been for Castrose lunging forward and taking Bailey's weight, they both would have fallen.

"What happened?" Clayton squeaked, worry thrumming through him. He eyed his mate, looking for signs of injury. "Is he okay?"

"I'm sure he'll be fine," Castrose replied, although he didn't sound very convincing.

Eion eased Clayton to the side as Castrose swung Bailey into his arms. "He probably just got some of his memories back," he guessed, his voice soothing. "It was probably just a shock."

Clayton nibbled his bottom lip as he took in his unconscious lover in his brother's arms.

So annoying.

"Good shock or bad shock?" he couldn't help but ask.

"Probably bad," Castrose grumbled. "Gather your stuff, and let's go."

As Castrose began moving, the sweatshirt began to slip, since Bailey was no longer holding it.

"Damn it all, Cass," Eion snapped, jumping forward. "Wrap the damn sweatshirt around his waist. I don't need you seein' the man's willie any more than Clayton does."

"Sorry," Castrose muttered, annoyance in his tone and expression. "Not my fault."

Eion rolled his eyes as he grabbed the sweatshirt.

Unable to help himself, Clayton growled and snatched the shirt from the man. "Mine." Then he carefully tucked the sweatshirt around his man's waist, even pushing one of the arms between his legs. He noticed Castrose and Eion both looking pointedly in other directions.

Good.

Once Clayton felt certain the sweatshirt securely hid Bailey's groin, he stepped back. As much as he didn't want to allow his shifter out of his sight—and Clayton completely considered him a shifter, regardless of how it came about—he turned to gather his stuff while saying, "You can head down, if you want. I'll be right behind you."

Castrose nodded. "Will you escort him, Eion?"

"Sure," his brother's wolf shifter mate replied.

Clayton scoffed softly as he knelt and began gathering their interrupted meal. Even as he mentally acknowledged that it was a big brother thing—and Castrose was still getting over the close call on Clayton's life the prior year—it still irked him to be left a babysitter.

Oh well.

Clayton focused on shoving everything back into his bag. Then he slipped his sandals back on his feet and slung the strap over his shoulder. As he made his way out of the cave, he shivered.

The mountain air had grown chilly, far too chilly for his skinny frame to go shirtless. Unfortunately, he didn't have anything else. To his surprise, Eion slipped off his flannel overshirt and held it out to him.

Clayton smiled gratefully as he took the shirt and handed over his bag, freeing his hands to don the soft item.

"Your brother just worries about you," Eion commented softly as they started down the trail together. He tapped his elbow into Clayton's as he added, "First he thought you were dead, then kidnapped, only to find you alive and well and had to learn about a whole new world."

"I know," Clayton replied softly, hurrying down the trail. His brother had been a sniper in the Swedish military and could move damn fast, even carrying a maybe-one-hundred-eighty-pound man. "But why isn't he happy that I found my mate? Even if he didn't start out as a shifter? He'll learn, and we'll figure out how to be together."

Jogging beside him, Eion chuckled softly. "Probably because he doesn't know anything about Bailey." He shrugged. "Only what we've been told by Ronan, but he hasn't had a close relationship with his brother in years." Grimacing, Eion added, "Being in the military can do that to a person. Their brothers-in-arms become their family if they're not careful."

Clayton thought about that, nodding. When Castrose had gone into the military, he and Clayton had made a promise to each other. They'd been the only family they'd had left, so they'd vowed to always stay in touch, even if it was the old-fashioned way of writing letters. It had been hard sometimes, and there had been gaps in correspondence, but they'd done it.

"It's going to be difficult for Castrose to hand over my care to another man," Clayton mused, dropping to a walk as he began panting for breath. "He's always been in that role, and now it's being taken away."

"You'll work through it," Eion claimed with a wink. "Brothers always do."

Clayton wheezed a chuckle, still struggling to breathe. He knew Eion had several brothers and a couple of sisters. Clayton couldn't imagine being part of such a large family, even though Eion's did try to include him as often as Clayton would let them.

Due to being such a homebody, Clayton still struggled with that.

I wonder what Bailey is like.

Too out of breath from hurrying to carry on much of a conversation, Clayton fell into silence. He figured Eion understood because the shifter didn't try to engage him. Instead, he kept pace while scanning the area around them.

When the trees parted to reveal the clearing making up not only Clayton's front yard but Beta Dixon and his mate, Helsinki's back yard, he saw the beta standing on the back deck. When Clayton had first met the large, blond male, he'd been so disappointed that the wolf shifter wasn't his mate. After all, Dixon was hot.

Even though the shifter wasn't his mate, he'd still cleared a huge area behind his cabin. He'd built a large workshop with an apartment over it. There was even an awesome second-story deck, where Clayton loved to have his morning coffee . . . assuming he'd slept.

My own mate is so much hotter — lean, toned, and sexy as hell.

When Dixon spotted them exiting the forest, he lifted a hand and beckoned.

Clayton glanced toward his shop, wondering if Castrose had taken his mate there, instead.

"Come on, Clayton," Dixon hollered. "Bailey's in my spare room."

Picking up his pace once more, Clayton crossed to the beta wolf shifter. "Why didn't my brother take him to my place?" he called curiously. "I mean, since he's my mate."

Dixon crossed his arms over his chest and narrowed his eyes. "First, because that's a hell of a lot of steps for all of us to get up and down while we question him," he stated bluntly. "Second, because we don't know the man or if he'll be able to control his cat. Last time he woke up, he ran away, so he needs to be monitored."

Clayton wanted to counter all the wolf shifter's claims, but he knew better than to say anything against the beta's words. After all, they were probably relayed from Alpha Declan. On top of that, Clayton knew Dixon to be a forceful but fair shifter who cared about everyone under his protection.

"Um, can I see him, please?" Clayton really wanted to know his shifter was safe.

Dixon reached out and gently touched the side of Clayton's neck. Carefully, he eased Eion's shirt over a little. He cocked his head as he arched one brow, obviously taking in the claiming mark.

With a smirk, Dixon murmured, "You move fast." Then he released him and pointed toward Clayton's home. "My advice, don't go see your mate wearing another man's shirt and scent."

Clayton gaped for an instant, then nodded swiftly. "Right. Shifters are territorial."

"Yes," Dixon replied. "Even confused and newly made ones." With a wry smile, he told him, "I heard what happened to Detective Lyle Sullivan when he first came awake after being changed."

Nodding once more, Clayton turned and hurried across the lawn. As he moved, he undid the buttons holding Eion's shirt together and slipped it from his shoulders, allowing it to drop to the ground. "Thanks, Eion!" he hollered before forcing his tired legs to bound up the outdoor stairs to his apartment. He heard his brother's mate laugh before the door closed behind him.

Glancing around his home as he headed to his bedroom, Clayton grimaced. He supposed it was a good thing that they hadn't brought Bailey there. His place was sort of a mess. There were dirty dishes in the sink and on the counter. Paper notes with his scribbles were scattered over almost every surface. There were also clothes strewn about. Clayton had been too wrapped up in his next invention to care about where things ended up.

Clayton vowed to clean up the place for when he was allowed to bring Bailey home.

Damn. I hope he doesn't mind moving here.

Clayton really liked his new space and his new friends.

Stopping in the bathroom, Clayton grabbed the washcloth from the shower. He turned on the hot water and shifted from foot to foot impatiently as he waited for it to heat. Fortunately, he had one of those fancy, tankless heat-on-demand water heaters, so it only took a few seconds. After wringing out the cloth, he wiped down his neck, torso, and pits.

One thing could be said for the wolf shifters, they seemed to have a fantastic grasp of finances. Their people could spare no expense when building homes.

Doing his best to clean away Eion's scent on his chest, Clayton finished cleaning himself. He dried off a little haphazardly as he headed to the bedroom. Then he grabbed a fresh sweatshirt and tugged it over his head.

Even before his head was through the hole, Clayton was moving back toward his front door. He hurried back down the stairs to see Castrose and Eion waiting for him on Dixon's back deck. Taking in their concerned expressions, Clayton slowed his steps.

"Is everything okay?" Clayton asked as soon as he thought they could hear him. "Is it Bailey?"

Castrose clamped a hand on the back of his neck and pulled him into a short embrace. "Sort of, but I'm sure the doc will get him sorted."

Peering up the six-inch difference in their heights, Clayton frowned at his brother. "Well, what is it then?"

Grimacing, Castrose told him, "Well, Bailey woke up again, and he shifted back into a cat." He shook his head as he continued, "Dixon managed to keep him from going out the window again, and right now, they're squared off in the bedroom with Bailey on top of a bookshelf and Dixon keeping him treed, so to speak."

"Poor Bailey!" Clayton cried, yanking away from Castrose and heading toward the door.

"Wait." Castrose grabbed his upper arm, stalling his movements. "You can't go in there. It's dangerous."

Clayton attempted to pull from Castrose's grip, but his brother held him fast. "Let go," he ordered, glaring.

Castrose shook his head. "Like I said. It's dangerous."

"Not to me," Clayton countered. "He's my mate."

"We don't know how much control he has while in cat form," Castrose stated. "He might attack you by mistake."

Clayton blew a raspberry as he shook his head. "I met him first in cat form, remember? He won't hurt me."

"But—"

"Castrose." Eion rested his hand on Castrose's wrist. "We don't keep mates apart. Not unless there is a clear threat." His expression turned serious. "Clayton's presence should help."

"*Should*," Castrose rumbled, clearly torn. "But we don't know for certain."

"And we'll be right there to keep him safe, if need be," Eion reminded. "Now, let's all go."

While Castrose clearly didn't like the idea, judging by his clenched jaw, he still gave in to his mate. He released Clayton's arm, then reached beyond him and opened the sliding glass door.

Clayton wasted no time in hurrying to the guest bedroom. He'd lived with Dixon for a couple of months while the pack had built his workshop and home, so he knew the layout. He'd never been in the master suite, but the rest of the house was familiar, even with Helsinki's added touches.

Standing in the middle of the room was Dixon in his pale-blond wolf form. The canine shifter stood ready, his body slightly tensed. His ears were forward, and he stared up to the left.

Following the shifter's attention, Clayton peered up at the bookshelf. He bit his bottom lip because his first inclination was to laugh. He didn't know how Bailey had managed to cram his large feline body between the top of the bookshelf and the ceiling, but he'd done it.

Bailey lay crouched at the top, his back pressed against the ceiling, peering intently at Dixon with his lips curled away from his canines. A low growl rumbled from him.

As soon as Clayton took a step further into the room, the noise stopped. The cheetah's head swiveled to focus on him. A soft mewling noise, something that sounded distinctly like distress, erupted from the shifter.

"Hey, Bailey," Clayton murmured, smiling at his lover. "It's safe here. I promise." He lifted a hand and beckoned. "Will you come down, please? These guys can help. Remember?"

The feline glanced from Clayton to Dixon and back again, clearly uncertain.

Clayton grinned and pointed at Dixon. "That's Beta Dixon Holsteen. He's second-in-command of the Stone Ridge wolf pack. This is his home." Moving his hand to point outside, he continued, "My home is right back there. They built it for me, so I'd have plenty of space to work on my bombs. I can't wait to show it to you."

After a bit of awkward maneuvering, Bailey leaped to the floor. He immediately lunged at Clayton.

Castrose jumped forward as if to intervene, but he was too slow.

Bailey pressed into Clayton's legs, herding him away from everyone else. He ended up in the corner, with Bailey between him and the rest of those in the room.

Gently, Clayton placed his hand on Bailey's shoulder and rubbed, enjoying the soft fur beneath his fingers. "It's okay," he repeated. "Promise."

While Bailey stilled under Clayton's touch, he didn't shift, and he didn't move from his guarding position.

Clayton glanced around at everyone and shrugged. "Um,

now what?"

Castrose didn't appear happy, but he didn't offer an answer, either. Dixon sat on his haunches and tilted his head a little. Although he looked relaxed, Clayton bet he could jump into action in an instant.

"Well, I guess we wait until Bailey calms down," Eion stated.

The bang of the front door slamming open sounded through the room.

Bailey snarled and tensed.

"Dixon?" Clayton recognized Alpha Declan's voice. "Where are ye?"

Dixon yipped softly to answer the alpha.

The sound of several footsteps told everyone that the alpha wasn't alone.

Clayton felt Bailey damn near vibrate beneath his palms, so he petted him gently and whispered reassurances.

Alpha Declan appeared first, pausing just inside the doorway. He took everything in at a glance, arching one brow when he saw how Bailey protected Clayton.

Then another man appeared, someone older with a brace on his left knee. His clean-shaven face registered surprise as he stared at the cat.

"Bailey?" he rumbled. "Is that really you?"

CHAPTER FIVE

Bailey eyed the newcomer and realized he knew him — Ronan. Rumbling softly, he stared at his brother. He wondered if the man would still look at him the same way once he found out the truth.

Would Clayton?

Ronan grinned broadly. "It's good to see you out of bed, Bays," he rumbled deeply. "I've been so damn worried about you." Ronan continued to stare for a few heartbeats, then asked, "Will you shift so we can talk?"

Even though Bailey's newly woken, protective shifter instincts continued to scream at him to stay in cat form so he could better protect his mate, he knew there was so much to discuss.

Bailey thought about his human form, and that was all it took. He found it shocking how quickly and easily his body could change form. It didn't even truly hurt, feeling more like a really good stretch. Once Bailey achieved his human form, he knelt on the floor with one leg cocked up, hiding his nudity . . . sort of.

Yeah, that'll take some getting used to, too.

Peering around at everyone, Bailey blew out a long breath. He felt Clayton's hand on his shoulder and lifted one hand to rest it over the man's. Having never been in a relationship in his life, he knew the urge he felt to touch and please the man came from his new shifter genes, but that didn't make it any easier to deny them. Bailey didn't even want to try, either, which he found interesting and unsettling all at the same time.

"Hi, Ronan. It's good to see you, too," Bailey murmured, finding his tongue. "Um, how'd I end up here?"

I should have woken in a military hospital under the care of Doctor Winoan.

"That's a long story," the black man commented in a mild Irish accent, a wry smile curving his lips. "Eion, grab Bailey some sweatpants. Then we'll all sit down for a cup of coffee." Bailey's stomach rumbled, and the man added, "And food."

Bailey remembered meeting Eion and Castrose and gratefully took the sweats from the man. "Thank you," he murmured, rising to his feet to put them on.

As Bailey did that, the wolf who Clayton had called Dixon changed back to human form. He also took a pair of sweats from Eion and pulled them on.

Then the black man held out his hand. "I'm Alpha Declan McIntire. I lead the pack here."

After a second of hesitation, Bailey reached out and took the man's hand. He gave it a firm shake, but he knew better than to try to overpower the man. The presence in Bailey's mind that he recognized as his cat side saw the male as more dominant.

"Nice to meet you," Bailey replied, dipping his head a little in submission.

Alpha Declan nodded back, then turned and headed out of the room. Eion began to follow. Then he must have realized Castrose wasn't following, so he paused and grabbed his mate's hand, giving it a tug to get him moving.

Ronan limped the few steps between them and wrapped Bailey in a tight hug.

Bailey sank into his brother's embrace, carefully hugging him back, since he didn't yet know his own strength. "I'm so confused." Bailey whispered the admission. "And scared."

"Waking up to all these changes must be scary as hell," Ronan whispered back. "We're here to help. Don't worry."

Easing back a little, Bailey met Ronan's gaze squarely. "I expected some of these changes, Ronan. The shifting isn't what scares me."

Cocking his head, Ronan frowned. "What do you mean?"

"I . . . I signed up for this," Bailey admitted.

"What?" The disbelief was clear in Ronan's tone.

Then Bailey's stomach rumbled again. He had no idea when he'd shared food with Clayton in that cave, but his stomach definitely told him that it had been too long ago. His body ached for sustenance in a way he'd never before experienced.

"Why don't you come with me," Dixon stated, drawing both men's attention. He rested his hand on Bailey's neck and squeezed in a way that Bailey found oddly reassuring. "I bet there's a hell of a story here, and we need to hear it."

Bailey nodded. "Yes, sir."

"Not sir," Dixon countered, releasing him. "Dixon is fine unless we're at an official gathering with shifters not from our pack."

Nodding again, Bailey figured he would never be included in that.

"Let's go," Ronan urged, releasing him and beckoning at the same time. "Oh." He paused and held out his hand to Clayton. "Nice to officially meet you. I hear it's your bombs Prier used to level that military medical facility a couple of weeks ago."

Clayton grinned broadly as he shook Ronan's hand. "Yep. He said he had fun and pulled lots of info from their systems. They're still going through it." He reached out and took Bailey's hand. "I'm sure some of that research was used to help you."

Bailey felt his stomach clench, and not from hunger. "Someone blew up a military medical facility?"

Holy shit! Was it Winoan's?

"Yep," Dixon confirmed. "And some of the files helped the

doc fix the memory wipe they were doing on you."

Freezing midstride, Bailey almost fell over. Getting his balance, he gaped at Dixon. "Doctor Winoan was doing what?" He didn't want to believe it. "That's not what I agreed to."

Dixon narrowed his eyes, but all he said was, "Hmmm, let's go eat. Shifting is hungry work."

Bailey allowed Clayton to tug him forward again. His mind reeled as he tried to decide what he believed. Could these men actually be telling the truth? Surely his own brother would never lie to him about something so important.

"They'll do everything they can to explain," Clayton assured. "We'll get everything sorted."

"Okay."

Bailey didn't know what else to say. His life had been turned on its head for a second time in . . . however long he'd been awake.

And how long was I unconscious?

So many questions.

Following Clayton's urging, Bailey headed down a hallway into the main room of the place. It boasted a fairly open concept, allowing everyone in the living, dining, and kitchen to see each other. Clayton guided Bailey to a chair at the table, and he settled beside him. Ronan sat on the other side, with Castrose beside him and Eion leaning against his chair.

Alpha Declan sat at the head, and a small blond man Bailey vaguely recognized settled on his lap. "This is my mate, Doctor Lark Trystan," Declan told him.

Lark smiled at Bailey. "I'm sorry Drake and I freaked you out," he told him. "We didn't mean to. Honest. We were just clearing your system of some of the mind-altering drugs the military had dosed you with."

"They really did that?" Bailey asked softly. "They were trying to wipe my memory?"

He still had a hard time believing it.

"Afraid so," Lark replied with a grimace.

"Why would they do that?" Bailey muttered, although he didn't really expect an answer. "What about the rest of my team?"

"I do believe there's a shadow branch of the military trying to create their own shifter army," a slender man stated, sauntering in the room from the sliding back door. "Was your team held at the facility your brother removed you from?"

"I think we really need to start at the beginning, Prier," Dixon commented, placing several mugs on the table, then sliding them in front of everyone. "How do you like your coffee, Bailey?" he asked before moving back to the kitchen.

Just then, a huge strawberry blond-haired man lumbered in through the front door. He grinned broadly at Dixon and hurried to him. Dixon smiled back, lifting an arm toward him. The man stopped in Dixon's space, and Dixon cradled his nape, guiding him down for a welcome-looking kiss.

Bailey felt his cheeks heat a little at the open display. While his team had known he was bisexual, and Warren on his team had been, too, he'd never acted on it around them. Neither had Warren.

Instead, when on leave, he and Warren had occasionally waited until their friends had found a hook-up and had headed out before they would visit a different club.

"That's Helsinki, Dixon's mate," the stranger stated, settling to lounge in a chair opposite him. "And I'm Prier." He held out his hand. "Nice to meet you."

After shaking the guy's hand, Bailey realized he was getting a read on scents. He knew the guy was human, as was Lark, and Declan and Dixon scented of wolf. Helsinki, on the other hand, while definitely a shifter, was something else . . . something that made his cat a little bit nervous.

"And ye'll get used to the displays," Declan commented, patting his shoulder. "Mated paranormal couples aren't shy."

As if to emphasize his point, a clearly Native American

man walked in the back door and crossed to Prier. He cupped the human's jaw while bending at the waist. A second later, he sealed his lips over Prier's and laid a carnal, possessive-looking kiss to his lips.

"Because they do that a lot," Lark said with a snicker. Then he turned and pecked a kiss to Declan's, who smiled indulgently at him.

"Sooo, uh, a lot of couples here," Bailey mused softly, beginning to feel overwhelmed, and they hadn't even gotten to the explanations, yet.

"Yes," Declan confirmed. "My pack has been truly blessed." Then he pointed at the Native American who was taking a seat beside Prier. "And that's my head enforcer, Kajika."

Kajika just nodded at him, the smallest of smiles teasing the corner of his lips.

Dixon appeared with a coffee carafe. "So, coffee?"

Bailey nodded, sliding his mug closer to the shifter. As he watched Dixon fill the mug, he asked, "Is it rude to ask a shifter what kind of animal he shares his, um . . . body with?"

"Not when ye're amongst friends," Declan told him with an understanding smile. "Wondering about Helsinki?"

Bailey shifted in his seat uncomfortably. "Yeah." Picking up his mug, he brought it to his lips and blew softly over the steaming liquid. "And black is fine, thanks."

As Dixon poured everyone coffee—except Castrose, who shook his head—the shifter in question grinned broadly and placed a mug of hot chocolate before Clayton's brother instead. Then Helsinki returned to the stove in the kitchen. "Polar bear," he told Bailey. "And we call it sharing our spirit, not our body." Before turning back to the stove, Helsinki asked, "So why did you decide to be a guinea pig and let those guys work on ya? Did you know you'd end up a shifter?"

Bailey had known the question would be coming. Hunching his shoulders, he grimaced as he stared into his coffee. He tightened his hold on Clayton's hand, wondering if he would pull away once he found out the truth.

"I found propaganda videos on the scientists' servers," Prier commented idly. "If I'd seen them before meeting Grady, I probably would have agreed to just about anything to fight shifters." Curving his lips into a wry smile, he eyed his mate. "They paint you with a very dangerous brush, Injun."

"Good grief," Alpha Declan grumbled. "I thought we'd dealt with this already."

"When one group is shut down, another always seems to pop up," Dixon replied with a shake of his head. He leaned his hip against the counter. "So, you were shown videos about how we're dangerous and planning to wipe out all the humans and take over the world."

Surprised at how easily they were taking the news, Bailey nodded. "Yeah." He knew he needed to explain more, so he added, "The videos showed footage of shifters breaking into a hospital, killing all the unarmed people inside, and destroying equipment. Then the building blew up."

"How did ye know they were shifters?" Declan asked, his eyes narrowing.

"Uh, they crept in as animals. Three wolves, a tiger, and a bear," Bailey explained. "Then the bear turned into a human." He grimaced, adding, "I've known I was bi since I was seventeen, but I hope to never have to see that man's flabby ass ever again."

"Huh," Helsinki piped up from the kitchen where he was plating up a mountain of eggs. "I'm a polar bear, and our kind have a little extra around the middle, but I'd never call myself flabby." He handed the huge bowl to Dixon, then started flipping the sizzling strips of bacon in another pan. "What kind of bear was it? I didn't think there were any kind that got fatter than us."

"Um, a grizzly, actually," Bailey told them, confused as he eyed Helsinki. "And I wouldn't call you flabby, either."

The bear shifter wasn't trim and muscular like the wolves, but he wasn't fat by any means, either.

"Wait." Bailey glanced around at everyone. "Is it normal for a shifter to be"—he lifted his hand from his coffee mug and waved it absently as he searched for the right word—"fit?"

Dixon placed the bowl of eggs on the table, then headed toward the cupboard and started getting dishes.

Declan answered. "It's rare for a shifter to be what I would consider flabby," he mused. "Our metabolisms work so much faster that we can normally eat as much as we want and not worry about it."

"There are a few shifter breeds that carry a little extra weight around their waists," Lark added, pointing at Helsinki. "Like polar bears and elephants. Their animals require a little extra weight since they're so large."

Confused, Bailey admitted, "Because one of the wolves shifted later in the footage, and he was definitely not what I would call fit."

"I think the propaganda videos were faked," Prier stated flatly. "Although we have taken a number of facilities, they always seemed to be filled with guys with guns, scientists experimenting on shifters, and the shifters they're torturing."

"We certainly don't go into hospitals full of unarmed civilians," Declan stated, sounding offended. "Why the hell would we do that?"

Bailey took a swig of his coffee before answering, "Because if there are less people to help heal humans in the upcoming war, then more will die in the attacks."

"That's morbid," Dixon commented as he passed out

plates and silverware. "When are we supposed to begin this supposed attack on humanity?"

"Uh, that wasn't discussed," Bailey admitted. "But we were offered enhancement so we'd be ready." Grimacing, he added, "They warned us we might end up with shifting abilities, but they had an injection ready to control it, so we wouldn't end up a monster like, um . . ."

"Like us?" Kajika finished dryly, although a smirk curved his lips.

Bailey just nodded.

Helsinki placed a platter piled high with bacon on the table as well as one full of potatoes.

The fantastic scent of the food caused Bailey's mouth to water and his stomach to grumble. A glance outside, however, showed him the sun was setting.

"Uh, breakfast for dinner?" Bailey felt his cheeks heat as he realized how rude his outburst was. "Sorry."

Dixon chuckled as he grabbed a plate and began filling it. "It's never the wrong time for bacon and eggs." He held the spoon that had been in the eggs out to Bailey. "That's just a myth."

"O-Okay," Bailey replied.

"Bailey, why were you in the hospital?" Ronan asked softly. "Were you injured?"

As Bailey placed a dollop of eggs onto Clayton's plate, then his own, he told his brother, "No, General Sackett called my team into his office and offered us a special assignment." He glanced at the other man again before adding potatoes to both their plates. "It was top secret, for national security." Bailey held out the spoon, holding his brother's gaze. "You know how that goes."

Ronan sighed as he took the offered utensil. "Yeah. I know." Squeezing his brother's shoulder, he told him, "Guess it worked out for the best, though."

Peering at Clayton, who still held his hand and was struggling to eat with his left, Bailey smiled. "Yeah, it did."

CHAPTER SIX

"I hate to say it, but I think it's time to contact Agent Craigson," Alpha Declan stated with a sigh. "The CIA needs to get involved in this one."

Prier sneered. "I prefer vigilante."

"I know ye do." Declan chuckled, shaking his head. "But we went our own way many times, and these things keep popping up. We need the CIA to curtail their own people, or it'll just keep happening."

Heaving a put-upon sigh, Prier rolled his eyes. "Very well."

Kajika teased a fingertip over Prier's jaw and murmured, "I'll help you with distractions."

Prier growled softly and leaned toward Kajika, accepting a kiss from his shifter mate. "I love your distractions," he purred.

"Gentlemen," Alpha Declan rumbled, sounding amused. "Let's focus. Shall we?"

Grinning, Prier straightened. "Yes, Alpha." Then he began piling his plate with food.

"Do you want your hand so you can eat easier?" Bailey asked softly, squeezing his fingers.

Clayton shrugged as he awkwardly scooped up some eggs with his left hand. "It's okay." Smiling at Bailey, he admitted, "I like holding your hand."

Bailey's cheeks darkened a little even as he admitted, "I like holding your hand, too." His brows furrowed as he admitted, "Never held hands with anyone before. Is this normal?"

"Tactile contact with yer mate is a natural part of being a shifter," Alpha Declan explained, obviously having caught on to Bailey's confusion. "Ye'll want to touch often."

"You'll also have a nearly undeniable urge to take care of your mate's needs and see to their happiness." Dixon pointed at Clayton's plate. "Hence you fixing up Clayton's plate."

"Sex with your mate will always be epic," Prier told him with a lascivious grin. "And you'll never be tempted to cheat."

"Really?" Bailey's eyes widened, and he focused on Clayton. "Not that I'd ever want to be tempted to cheat."

"I know that's not what you meant," Clayton told him, snickering. "But it's nice to know, huh?"

Bailey nodded slowly. "Yeah." His expression turned wry. "It also explains why you were so open to accepting me, no questions asked."

"It helps that you're the hottest man I've ever met," Clayton deadpanned.

Shaking his head and smiling, Bailey obviously didn't believe Clayton.

That's okay. I'll just have to repeat it until he's convinced.

As they ate, Ronan explained how the military saying Bailey had refused to see any family while in the hospital had aroused their suspicions. Due to that, he'd found a way to break in and had secreted an unconscious Bailey from the place. Then he'd hidden him with an old army buddy while he'd ended up on the run.

Ronan finished by explaining how he'd run into Markus while hiding in the woods, his aggravated knee injury, and how Markus's people had been willing to help. Then he dropped one more bombshell.

"Mom, Dad, and Isabel are in the area, too," Ronan stated, holding Bailey's gaze. "They'd been told you were dead, and

I was in a military prison."

Bailey groaned, rubbing a hand over his face. "I can't believe our own people did that to us." His grip on Clayton tightened a smidge, telling Clayton how much he appreciated their connection. "Are they okay now? If they're here, I'm assuming they know I'm not dead, right? Should I go see them tonight?"

"We have a few more things to discuss before ye can see them," Declan stated, placing his fork on his plate. "Yer mother is a bit . . . bigoted." He pointed at where Bailey continued to hold Clayton's hand. "She has not been supportive of Ronan and Markus, but perhaps just having ye back from the dead will make the difference with you and Clayton."

"I'm not giving him up," Bailey declared, growling low in his throat. He let go of Clayton's hand, only to haul him onto his lap. "He's mine."

Clayton had never sat on another man's lap before, and he didn't find it very comfortable. Still, he knew his shifter needed the contact, so he didn't struggle. Rubbing his palm over Bailey's chest, Clayton did his best to try to soothe the man.

Alpha Declan lifted his hand, palm out in placation. "None of us would ever suggest that," he told him. "Try to relax, Bailey. All I'm saying is we need to come up with a narrative that explains ye suddenly having a partner after being in a coma for nine months."

Bailey blew out a soft breath. At the same time, he dipped his head and pressed his nose against Clayton's neck. He nuzzled lightly as he drew in a noisy breath.

Understanding his shifter mate was using his scent to calm down, Clayton tipped his head to the side, offering more room. At the same time, he cast a tentative smile Markus's way and commented, "So, the in-laws aren't too good, huh?"

Markus smirked. Ronan's wolf shifter mate had arrived

halfway through the meal. "Just the mother-in-law. Their father is a kind and understanding man, and their sister is quite charming."

Lifting his head, Bailey turned his attention to Ronan. "How did they take the news that I wasn't dead?" He frowned. "Still can't believe all the lies my superiors spread. The military is supposed to be the good guys."

"Hopefully, it's just a rogue sect," Declan stated.

"Everyone cried like you'd expect," Ronan added with a smile. "But they were happy tears."

Bailey nodded again. "Well, the partner is easy enough," he began slowly. "I knew Mom was less than accepting, but now that I'm essentially back from the dead, I refuse to hide the love of my life any longer."

When Bailey peered down at him and teased his fingers through Clayton's hair, a tingle went up his spine. He was surprised at the intensity of the shifter's gaze and thought maybe, just maybe, he really did see love within the depths of his eyes. Uncertain what to say, he closed his eyes and nuzzled into his lover's touch, deciding maybe lap-sitting wasn't so bad. After all, he couldn't think of anything better than being held by his sexy shifter.

"Your mother also doesn't know about shifters, so you can't discuss it with your family," Dixon warned, drawing their attention. "You can never tell anyone."

"Understandable, Dixon," Bailey replied, turning his focus to the beta. "Them knowing would just paint a cross-hairs on them anyway. They're better off not knowing."

Alpha Declan smiled. "Glad ye agree. Now then, finish yer food. I canna imagine how starving ye are after being turned into a shifter and being in a coma for nine months. Ye must still be famished."

Bailey slid his plate closer and did as he'd been bid, but he didn't allow Clayton to slip into his own seat. Instead, he drew Clayton's plate closer to them, too.

"Sorry," Bailey mumbled, his brows furrowing. "I don't think I can put you down, yet."

Clayton smiled back at him. "It's fine. We'll make it work."

"Your shifter instincts and needs are a little ramped up right now," Kajika explained. "Between figuring them out for the first time and finding your mate, you'll need to stay close to each other for a while." With a wink, he added, "Although, since night is coming, I don't see that as going to be a problem."

Clayton felt his cheeks heat, and he peered at Bailey through his lashes. "You'll stay with me, won't you?"

Appearing pleased, Bailey grinned. "Just try to tear me away."

Relief filled Clayton, and he returned to eating.

As Bailey snagged a piece of bacon, he focused on Prier. "You mentioned files at this place you destroyed," he began slowly, sounding thoughtful. "Was there anything on my teammates?"

"What are their names?" Prier asked, relaxing in his seat with his coffee mug cradled between his palms.

"Warren Berger, David Preston, Miles Philson, and Crew Kester," Bailey rattled off.

Prier shook his head. "Guess I shouldn't have asked that. Sorry. Instinct."

"What do you mean?" Bailey asked, his grip tightening a little.

"Each patient's name was converted into a four-digit experiment number," Prier explained, tapping his forefinger on his coffee mug. "Yours was ZX-32. What I can tell you is the day after Ronan smuggled you out of that place, there were four *experiments*" — he lifted his fingers and made air quotes — "that were transferred out of the facility." With a growl, Prier added, "But I don't know where they went. We're still searching."

"If they're doing to them what they were doing to me, I'd like to find them and help them," Bailey told everyone firmly. "Maybe I can help. Where was the facility you took out?"

"A small town south of Des Moines, Iowa," Dixon answered, pushing his empty plate farther away from him on the bar. Then he placed an arm around Helsinki's shoulders. His mate sat on a nearby stool, continuing to finish up his own meal. "Do you remember that place?"

Grimacing with a sigh, Bailey nodded. "Yeah, that was where we were flown. Des Moines, I mean." He peered around at everyone, adding, "When we got off the plane, we were placed in the back of a box van that didn't have windows. We drove for almost forty minutes, so I guess, technically, that could have been in any direction."

"I'll double-check the area," Prier promised. "Just in case we missed something."

"How often does that happen?" Declan asked, teasing.

Prier scoffed. "In my original line of work? Never. That would have been deadly."

Declan chuckled. "As I thought."

"What did you used to do?" Bailey asked curiously.

With a toothy grin, Prier answered, "Assassin."

Bailey tensed, then relaxed again. "Okay."

"Wait." Ronan touched Bailey's forearm. "In the bedroom, you mentioned a name. Uh, Winoan. Who is that?"

"Yes." Prier drew the word out. "Who *is* that?"

Bailey finished chewing his bite of bacon before responding. "General Sackett introduced us after we agreed to secrecy," he told everyone. "He was introduced as Doctor Winoan, and he accompanied us from then on, as well as a half a dozen MPs." Rubbing his hand up and down Clayton's arm in an absent way, Bailey finished, "We weren't even asked to get gear or a go-bag."

"Well, that doesn't sound fishy," Ronan commented dryly.

"I knew it was," Bailey stated. "I could tell by the way all the guys were exchanging covert looks and not talking that they felt the same way." He shrugged. "But we'd given our word, and that was that."

Ronan rubbed Bailey's back. "I get it. I do."

Clayton figured Ronan did, too. The man had been in the military, too, until a roadside bomb had messed up his knee and thigh. He'd been given an honorable medical discharge and shown the door.

"Soooo, General Sackett and Doctor Winoan." Prier rose from his seat, a huge grin spreading over his lean features. "Thanks for a great new direction to look."

In the next instant, he was gone, Kajika going with him after tipping his chin respectfully to Alpha Declan.

Dixon chuckled. "He looked excited."

"Which normally means we're going to end up sending our people into a dangerous situation," Alpha Declan commented, suddenly sounding sad. "I'm so tired of prejudice."

"It's rampant in every society," Dixon stated sagely. "We'll always be facing it in one way or another."

Alpha Declan heaved out a breath. "I know." Then he pulled out his cell phone and placed it on the table before him. "Quiet, everyone, unless I ask ye to speak."

After everyone nodded, Alpha Declan made a call and put his phone on speaker. The sound of the line ringing came through.

For an instant, Clayton wondered why the phone company insisted on continuing to use that particular ringing noise even though few people actually had landlines any longer.

Must just be standard issue.

Then a deep voice answered. "Agent Craigson."

"Good evening, Agent Craigson," Declan greeted. "Thank ye for taking my call."

There was silence on the line for one heartbeat, two, then Craigson commented, "For a second, I didn't believe my phone's readout, Alpha Declan."

"I can believe that," the alpha replied. "It's been nearly seven years."

"I'd hoped no news was good news," the agent stated. "That's not the case, though. Is it?"

Declan sighed softly. "I'm afraid not. We've just been a bit more . . . discreet."

Craigson scoffed. "That's not something you should be telling me."

"I'm afraid I must," Declan countered. "We've run into quite a bit of a mess."

"A shifter didn't go public, did they?" Concern crept into Craigson's tone. "I haven't heard anything."

"Nothing that dire . . . maybe." Declan didn't sound completely certain. "Is the CIA aware of a shadow branch of the military continuing experiments on shifters and soldiers?"

"Fuck."

Declan growled softly. "I'll take that as a no."

"No," Craigson replied resolutely. "Do you know who?"

"We have a couple of names." Then Declan hesitated before admitting, "And a destroyed location. Ye know some of my people."

Craigson's heavy sigh came through the line. "Yes, I know some of your people." There was a soft sound of rustling. Then he stated, "Got a pen. Hit me with the details."

"Ye're really not going to like them," Declan warned.

"If you're coming to me with them, I bet it's really bad."

Clayton bit his bottom lip. That Craigson guy was smart.

"The ones doing the experiments are in the US military," Declan revealed. "We've already removed a few people, but more just keep cropping up. We need to discover the head of the snake."

"Our military?" Craigson repeated. "Damn." After another heaved sigh, he ordered, "Okay. Lay it on me."

Declan did. He shared information about people they'd taken out that Clayton hadn't even heard of. Through it all, the others stayed silent, although there were a lot of looks exchanged. Finally, Declan culminated with Bailey's information.

"I really wish you would have contacted me sooner," Craigson admitted. "We could have been working to shut this down for years." Sounding frustrated, he added, "Hell, we could have had it knocked out already."

"I have a question now," Declan stated, ignoring Craigson's ire. "Is yer new director better than the last one?"

Craigson barked a laugh. "Ah, so that's why you didn't contact us."

"Indeed," Declan replied. "I have no wish to work with homophobes."

"Well, my current director is dating a man three years his junior, so I think you're good there."

"Glad to hear it."

Chapter Seven

Bailey couldn't believe how everything had gone down with the pack, although the relief his cat felt had almost sent him sagging to the floor. They hadn't condemned him because of why he'd signed up. Instead, they'd offered understanding, had helped him heal, and they were even going to help him locate his squad.

I hope we find them before their memories are erased.

"It's real good to have you back, Bays," Ronan stated, pulling him into another hug. "Rest tonight. Recuperate." His expression turned wry as he told him, "The folks visit you every other day. This is your reprieve."

"Is Mom really that bad?" Bailey asked warily.

Ronan nodded. "When I first went to get them, we were attacked in the house." He eased his hold and glanced over his shoulder at a waiting Markus. "Markus shifted and took a bullet meant for Dad, and Mom still called him a monster."

"Shit, seriously?" Bailey focused on his brother's partner. "Are you okay?"

Markus smiled. "I'm fine. Your sister is taking pre-vet classes, and she pulled the bullet out."

"She is? Damn." Then a thought hit Bailey. "But Declan said that I can't disclose that I'm a shifter to our family. Why, if they already know?"

Clearing his throat, Ronan stepped back and rubbed the back of his neck. "Well, uh . . . we had Mom's memory altered."

Gaping, Bailey shook his head. As Ronan grimaced and

nodded, he demanded, "If they can alter Mom's memories, how do you know our memories haven't been changed in some way? What if—"

"Whoa, whoa," Ronan rumbled, resting his hands on Bailey's shoulders. "Shifters can't alter memories. Alpha Declan asked a vampire friend to do it."

"Vampires are real?" Bailey hissed, his head swimming. "But—"

How do people not know this?

Ronan lightly massaged Bailey's shoulders, but it was the slender fingers rubbing up and down his back as well as the hand taking his own that pulled Bailey back from the edge. He already recognized Clayton's touch. The animal he now shared his mind with would know it anywhere.

My mate. That couldn't be a fabrication. The cat I turn into can't be faked.

"A lot of things that most people think are myth or legend are actually real," Clayton whispered. "The stories have to come from somewhere." His brows furrowed. "Although, many of the stories aren't accurate."

Bailey blew out a breath before wrapping his arms around Clayton and pulling him close. "Okay. So vampires." Huffing a sigh, he stared at Ronan. "Vampires are real, and they can alter people's memories." Bailey shook his head as he muttered, "And they altered Mom's, so she doesn't know about shifters anymore?"

Ronan nodded. "She really couldn't handle it."

"And Dad and Isabel?" Bailey pressed.

"They know," Ronan confirmed. "But we have to be careful when and where we discuss it because we can't have Mom finding out again."

Bailey nodded. "Okay." He held his brother's gaze. "I understand. No paranormal talk around Mom, and we're going to deal with some bigotry." Peering into the gorgeous blue eyes of the man in his arms, Bailey murmured, "I'm sorry in advance."

Clayton scoffed and rolled those pretty eyes. "How other people behave is not your fault." Smiling up at him, he added, "We'll make it work."

As Bailey contemplated taking Clayton's lips, a yawn overtook him.

Chuckling, Ronan patted him on the back. "I'll see you tomorrow." With a wink and a smirk, he stated, "Enjoy your evening, Bays."

Bailey felt his face heat as he watched Ronan limp away from him. Markus was instantly at his side, wrapping his arm around his waist. The shifter offered his brother support as they headed to the front door.

Clayton guided Bailey in the opposite direction, moving to the rear sliding door.

"Thank you for supper, Dixon," Bailey said as they passed the pair. They were in the kitchen, cleaning, and he paused. "Can we help before we go?"

Dixon snorted and shook his head. "Get out of here, guys, and don't look back." A hungry smile curved his lips as he peered at Helsinki. "As soon as you're out the door, I'm gonna fuck my mate over the kitchen counter."

Instead of seeming upset by the crass comment, Helsinki's nostrils flared, and his eyes widened. "Yes, please," he murmured breathily.

Bailey blurted, "Is everyone so open about sex here?"

Dixon refocused on him, and he shrugged. "This pack has truly been blessed with a large amount of fated mates, so . . . yeah. It's something you'll have to get used to."

"Because you're assuming I'm staying here?" Bailey had noticed the way others spoke and had understood the insinuation.

Not even trying to be discreet, Dixon nodded. "Of course." He lifted his hand and began ticking off on his fingers. "First, we can protect you from the assholes who experimented on you. And make no mistake, they'll definitely try to get you back." His second finger went up. "Your family is here." Another digit lifted. "And most importantly, Clayton is here, and it's not safe for him to leave."

Bailey focused on Clayton. "Really? Not safe?" His sudden need to check outside confused the hell out of him. "Why?"

Clayton shrugged his slender shoulders, and his expression turned guarded. "I told you I'm a bomb maker."

"We didn't really discuss that, huh?" Bailey pointed out. Tightening his hold on Clayton's fingers, he tugged him close again. "Are you a wanted man, Clay?"

"Um, technically, my brother's the wanted man," Clayton explained uncomfortably. "Because he was the one in the military, and we traded on his name." Scoffing, he added, "Who'd buy a bomb from some random geek, right?"

Dixon frowned at Clayton. "He needs to know, Clay," he pointed out. "He shared about the experiments with us, remember?"

Sighing and rolling his eyes dramatically, Clayton muttered, "Fine." Then he met Bailey's gaze and stated, "We're technically wanted in thirteen countries and almost got caught in Romania because I didn't realize one of the communication avenues Castrose and I used was compromised." Lifting his hands in a half-shrug, Clayton finished, "These guys found our hideout, saved me, and my brother tracked me here and found his mate, and now, so have I."

Bailey nodded in understanding. "Even if you weren't a wanted man" — he scowled at his mate for an instant — "and we'll discuss which of your actions made you wanted" — before once more smiling at him — "I'd be just fine with staying here."

Clayton sighed in relief, and Bailey felt like he'd just done something great.

This mating thing is so weird.

"Great. Now get out of here."

Following Dixon's order, Bailey pushed Clayton gently toward the door. "Come on, cute Clay." He winked. "Show me this home these guys built for you."

Grinning widely, Clayton tugged his hand and started moving faster. He hurried behind his lover, eager to be alone once more.

Outside, the darkness was nearly absolute with only a thin sliver of the moon shining down upon them. The cool mountain air sent a shiver through his body, clad only in sweatpants. He was reminded that he didn't even have a pair of shoes.

Bailey wondered if his apartment was being watched. Then it occurred to him that it was on the base. Surely his quarters would have been packed up, stored, tossed, or given to his parents, and the place would have been assigned to some other government lackey.

Damn, what a cynical thought. Too bad it's probably true.

Pushing the thoughts from his mind — he would find out what happened to his stuff later — he focused on Clayton and the tall structure they approached. It stood a little higher than the average two-story building with plenty of windows for the top floor, which was obviously an apartment. The bottom floor had more of a warehouse feel to it, with long windows set higher up on the walls, affording a bit of privacy mixed with ventilation.

Clayton led the way to an exterior set of stairs leading to a small deck and a second-story door. At the top, the view — even in the dark — appeared spectacular. Bailey would bet it was the perfect place to sit and drink coffee in the morning and admire the nearby mountain peaks.

As Clayton opened the door, he peered over his shoulder and offered Bailey a shy smile. "Do you want to shower with me?"

Bailey groaned softly as the idea of a wet, soapy Clayton

filled his mind. "Nothing would make me happier," he told his lover, looking forward to exploring his mate once more.

"I love when you look at me like that," Clayton admitted.

"Good," Bailey replied. Sweeping his gaze over Clayton, he added, "Because I can't help it and don't want to try."

Clayton grinned happily, not bothering to turn on the lights as he led the way through the open-concept area. Bailey's sharp, shifter eyes made out a slightly messy kitchen with a bit of clutter on the coffee table in the living room. The dining room table had papers strewn across it.

Bailey smiled to himself, liking the lived-in space. He'd always thought his apartment had a sparse air to it. This place felt like a home.

"It's only a one-bedroom," Clayton explained, glancing at him over his shoulder. He nibbled his bottom lip for a second before saying, "I hope it's not presumptuous to hope you're going to sleep in my bed with me." Then Clayton frowned. "I should change the sheets. It's been a while since I did it. I get distracted with my projects and don't remember some of the more mundane stuff."

"I can help you with that," Bailey offered with a grin. "One of the things the military teaches is cleanliness." As they entered the bedroom, he inhaled deeply and groaned again. "Although, sleeping in sheets saturated with your scent sounds . . ." Bailey hummed again. "Heavenly."

Then another yawn caught him, causing his jaw to crack.

"You've had a busy day, Bailey," Clayton commented. "Let's get you cleaned up and relaxed."

Bailey nodded, continuing to follow Clayton. The darkness, the bed, and his senses flooded with his lover's scent were creating odd, dual sensations within him. He wanted to grab Clayton, drag him to the bed, and curl up around him, assuring he was safe and secure while they slept. He also wanted to fuck him through the mattress, but he didn't know if he had the energy to do it justice.

"You're kinda dead on your feet," Clayton pointed out, tugging him into a spacious bathroom and flipping on the light. "Let me clean you."

Squinting in the sudden brightness, Bailey glanced around the space. The jetted tub would feel amazing on tired muscles after a workout — or a run. His lover leaned over and turned the water on in a spacious, dual-headed, tile-lined shower. Heat quickly began to fill the space.

Bailey had just enough presence of mind to push down his sweats and kick them off.

When Clayton turned back to face him, he sucked in a sharp breath. His eyes widened, and he swept a hungry look down, then back up, Bailey's body. His lips parted in an *oh* as he mouthed, *wow*.

Smug satisfaction flooded Bailey, and his body responded to his mate's reaction. His blood flowed south, and his prick thickened. Within seconds, he sported a throbbing erection that begged for attention.

Groaning, Bailey gripped his shaft and jacked lightly. "And I love the way you look at me," he rumbled, stalking forward. "But you're overdressed."

Bailey gripped the hem of Clayton's shirt and pulled it up and off, dropping it to the floor. Recalling doing this once before, he anticipated what he would reveal. Opening Clayton's fly, he grinned when he saw his lover had gone commando, skipping his underwear in a mad dash to cover himself in the cave.

Skimming his fingertips up the length of the erection separating the flaps, Bailey admired Clayton's twitching length. His lover was long in proportion to his height, but slender. He would burrow so deep inside Bailey's body.

Bailey clenched his chute muscles in anticipation. It had

been over a decade since he'd bottomed, but he looked forward to the day it would happen. He wanted to experience everything with Clayton.

When another yawn escaped Bailey, he returned his focus to undressing his lover. He helped him out of his sandals, then tugged his jeans off of him. Straightening, he held out his hand, palm up.

Smiling, feeling happier than he could remember in a long time, Bailey led Clayton into the exquisite shower. The feel of the hot water flowing over his body sent a fresh wash of fatigue through him. He sighed deeply and rested one forearm on the wall while hanging his head. That didn't stop Bailey from sliding his other arm around Clayton's slender waist and tugging him flush against him.

"Bailey?"

Smiling at the concern he heard in Clayton's voice, Bailey murmured, "Just give me a sec. This water feels so damn good, cute Clay."

"Just relax, Bay," Clayton purred, easing from his hold. "I'll take care of everything."

At first, Bailey resisted releasing Clayton, but his mate insisted. He allowed his lover to turn him so he could rest both forearms on the tile. Hanging his head, he found himself in the perfect position for the water to pour over his head and shoulders.

Bailey still cracked open his eyelids just enough to see but not so much that he would get water in his eyes. In his peripheral, he saw Clayton grab a bottle of body wash and a loofah, which made him smile. His lover poured a healthy dollop of liquid onto the poof and put the bottle back before working up a lather.

When Clayton rested it on Bailey's upper back and began stroking down his torso, he let out a contented sigh. The light rasp felt delicious, as did the fact that his lover used his other hand to skim his fingers over his ribcage. Clayton's hands were like magic, melting away every inch of tension in Bailey's body.

Clayton worked down his body, pausing an instant at the swells of Bailey's ass. Sensing his mate's hesitation, he widened his stance a little in invitation. His lover took him up on that and began massaging his ass cheeks.

Groaning softly, Bailey moved into Clayton's petting touches. His dick twitched, but he resisted the urge to grip himself. He hissed with pleasure when Clayton slid the loofah between his legs to clean his most hidden areas.

As Clayton moved the loofah lower with one hand, he kept his thumb between his cheeks. He applied light pressure to Bailey's hole, tearing a moan from his lips.

Obviously taking that as a sign, Clayton gently breached Bailey's guardian muscle, sinking his finger in deep.

"Fuck, Clay," Bailey whined, widening his stance a bit more. "Been too long. So good."

"You're so tight and hot," Clayton whispered before placing a sucking kiss to the base of Bailey's spine. "Can't wait to feel you someday."

"Yessss," Bailey hissed, and a shudder worked through him when Clayton gripped his shaft with his other hand.

Bailey didn't know when Clayton had dropped the loofah, and he didn't care. His tired body erupted with sensory overload as his mate worked his shaft. At the same time, Clayton managed to tease his prostate with spine-tingling glances.

If Bailey hadn't been in the throes of ecstasy, he would have been embarrassed at how swiftly his orgasm swamped him. He shuddered and twitched as his tight balls poured burst after burst of seed against the wall. His body trembled as he floated in bliss.

"Clay," Bailey murmured. "My mate. So good."

"Yes. All yours."

Upon hearing those words, Bailey began to shut down, barely comprehending anything else, safe and secure in the knowledge that he was with his mate.

CHAPTER EIGHT

Clayton had no idea how Bailey stayed on his feet. The man appeared half asleep, with his eyes nearly closed and doing whatever Clayton urged. He reveled in the faith Bailey had in him as he finished washing them both, then drying them.

Worried he wouldn't be able to get Bailey on his feet again if he urged him to sit in a chair, Clayton skipped changing the sheets. His shifter had seemed to appreciate the idea of sleeping with his scent anyway. He helped Bailey onto the bed, then pulled the sheet and blanket over him.

Before Clayton could cross to his dresser to grab a pair of sleep pants, Bailey grabbed his wrist and tugged. He toppled forward, half on top of his lover. In seconds, Clayton found himself tucked beside Bailey with the shifter's arms securely around him and his larger body spooned tightly against him.

"Relax and sleep, my mate," Bailey murmured into his ear while hugging him to his chest. "You're safe."

Clayton realized he'd completely tensed upon being manhandled. No one had ever done that to him before. Plus, he'd thought his lover almost asleep.

Blowing out a breath, Clayton forced his body to relax. He'd never slept with someone else before. Well, he'd holed up with Castrose while on the run, but his brother certainly didn't hold him like this.

"What's wrong?" Bailey whispered while nuzzling his neck.

"Never slept with anyone before," Clayton admitted.

When he felt Bailey's arms begin to loosen, he gripped his lover's wrists. "Please don't move." He did his best to cuddle back into his embrace, feeling his lover's soft penis nestle under his ass cheeks. "Just trying to get comfortable."

Bailey licked over Clayton's claiming mark, causing a wash of tingles to trickle down his torso. "Don't lie, my mate," his lover admonished. "What's really wrong?"

Clayton grimaced.

Right. Shifter noses.

Although, Clayton did wonder how Bailey knew about different scent markers when he'd only woken that morning.

Huh.

"I'm not sure," Clayton admitted, doing his best to relax. "Never slept with anyone before. Never slept without pants. Never been held like this." Turning his head, he tried to make out Bailey's expression in the dark room. "Would you be upset if I wanted to cuddle in a different position?"

Bailey smiled at him. "We can cuddle in any position you want as long as I still get to hold you," he told him. Then he teased his fingertips over Clayton's groin, skimming around the base of his prick. "And as long as you're naked." Humming, Bailey asked, "Did you get off in the shower, too?"

Clayton felt his cheeks heat as he began shifting position in Bailey's arms. "Yeah," he told him. "Thinking about fucking you someday while feeling your chute on my finger was totally hot."

"Good," Bailey replied, rolling to his back and urging Clayton to drape over his chest. "I'd hate to think I left you hanging." His brows furrowed as he added, "Even though, technically, I did."

"We're not keeping score," Clayton countered. Relaxing with his head on Bailey's shoulder, his arm over his torso, and his leg over his thighs, Clayton felt more relaxed. "This is better."

Bailey pressed a kiss to the top of Clayton's head. "We'll

find what works for us," he replied, his voice thick with impending sleep.

A few seconds later, Bailey's soft snores filled the room.

Clayton smiled, enjoying the rhythm of the chest moving beneath him, and quickly followed him into sleep.

The sensation of exquisite tingles shooting through his groin roused Clayton from a sound sleep. His cock throbbed, and he rocked his hips, rubbing his erection on the sheet beneath him. Talented fingers stretched his chute muscles and played with his prostate, and he moaned salaciously.

When a firm nudge bumped his prostate, Clayton gasped. A hot hand rubbed up his spine, then back down again. It settled on his hip, urging him to lift, to get his knees under him.

Clayton obeyed as he cracked his eyelids and took in Bailey's intense, hungry expression. His lover's focus was pinned to Clayton's ass where he was working him open. He spotted his tube of lube on the bed near his knee and realized Bailey must have gone searching, not that he minded at all if this was the result.

"You with me, my mate?" Bailey asked gruffly, sliding his focus up to meet his gaze. "Good."

His feral smile caused Clayton's gut to clench in anticipation. He didn't have to wait long.

Bailey eased his fingers from Clayton's body as he levered over him. His crown nudged his prepared hole, and Clayton pushed out, happy to accept what Bailey was packing. He sighed as he felt his lover's erection sink deep, deep into his body.

When Bailey bottomed out, he immediately reversed. His strokes were long and sure, sinking into him and retreating steadily. With each thrust, he prodded Clayton's prostate, stimulating him from the inside out.

Clayton went to grip the comforter in an attempt at leverage, but Bailey had other ideas. He threaded their fingers together, covering him completely. Burying his face in the crook of Clayton's shoulder, he began chanting one word in time with his thrusts.

He'd just made out that Bailey muttered, "Mine. Mine. Mine," with each rut when his lover began alternating sucking nips to his claiming mark amidst his chant.

Clayton's entire body went up in flames. From his head to his toes, he flushed hot, sweat pouring from him. Their bodies slid together, the slap of flesh hitting flesh as Bailey pounded into him filled the room like the best symphony.

"Come for me," Bailey urged, driving into his prostate. "Milk me. Wanna feel your body beg for my seed."

Flushing at the erotic image, Clayton felt his balls draw up as if wired to obey. He moaned Bailey's name as his orgasm washed over him. His seed sprayed from him in hard, bliss-inducing spurts.

"Yessss," Bailey hissed, slamming into him once, twice more. Then he sank deep and stilled.

Clayton had just enough time to register the heat of Bailey's seed coating his insides when his shifter's teeth sank into his neck. His gasp at the flash of pain immediately morphed into a contended moan. His body convulsed as a second ecstasy-filled release sent his senses soaring.

When Clayton's brain flickered back to life, he realized Bailey hadn't moved much. While he'd eased his teeth free, the shifter still had his dick inside his chute. Clayton recalled Bailey doing much the same thing last time and smiled, liking that his lover enjoyed staying connected so intimately.

"Sorry for waking you like that," Bailey mumbled, gentling his fingers' hold where they were twined. "Needed you."

"You can wake me like that any time you want," Clayton assured, peering over his shoulder at him. He spotted the way

Bailey's brows were furrowed and how he appeared slightly troubled. Recalling his shifter's near frantic chanting, Clayton asked, "Is something wrong?"

"Not wrong, exactly," Bailey replied softly. Gently, he urged them to the side, staying connected while moving away from the west spot. "Just had too many thoughts in my head when I woke."

"What thoughts?" Clayton pressed. When Bailey remained silent, he rubbed his palm up and down his lover's forearm as he stated, "Whatever it was, it upset you. I'd like to help, if I can."

Bailey let out a long sigh while clutching him close. "A mix of the whole situation," he began slowly.

Clayton guessed there was more to it than that, so he remained quiet, waiting.

His patience was rewarded when Bailey continued, "There's people after both of us, but I'm military, and we have support." He began rubbing his palm up and down Clayton's torso, pausing to rub his thumb around one nipple. "We'll deal with them."

"I'm not without skills, you know," Clayton reminded Bailey, doing his best to ignore the fresh wash of tingles his lover's petting was creating. "Castrose may have been the one in the military, but he taught me many things. I'm proficient with firearms, and I can wire a simple bomb in seconds."

Bailey flattened his palm over Clayton's belly. "I hear what you're saying, my mate, but I don't want to see you in a fight." A soft whine escaped him as he admitted, "Seeing you hurt would destroy me. I know it's fast, and I don't understand it myself, but it's true."

Clayton turned his head and gave Bailey an awkward kiss to his chin. "It's the shifter way, Bay. You don't need to explain." Snorting softly, he admitted, "And I really don't go looking for trouble. I'm just ready to defend myself if need be, is all."

"You getting hurt got me thinking about my family. My mom."

Hearing those surprising words, Clayton arched his brows. "I don't understand."

"What if my mother's words hurt you?" Bailey growled. "We know she's not going to be happy." Frowning, he asked, "What if something she says drives you away?" A whine entered his tone. "You're my mate."

Understanding filled Clayton. "So you needed to claim me again."

"Yeah," Bailey whispered. "It's irrational. I know that, but—"

"You're a shifter now," Clayton cut in. Shifting his hips, he eased Bailey's softened shaft from his body. As he turned to face his lover, he did his best to ignore the rush of cum he felt on his thighs.

That'll take some getting used to.

"You're learning and processing new instincts," Clayton reminded him as he settled on his side to face Bailey. Gripping his lover's hand, he brought it to his lips and kissed his knuckles. "And nothing your mother says will ever drive me away." Seeing Bailey's still-concerned expression, Clayton stated forcefully, "She'll *never* hold that kind of power over us, so I want you to get that idea out of your head right now."

Bailey stared deep into his eyes for several long seconds as if searching for the truth. His expression softened, and he let out a sigh. Finally, a smile curved his lips.

"Thanks for understanding," Bailey whispered.

Clayton returned the smile. "Trust me. It's no trouble. I've been learning about shifter society for a long while now." Then he waggled his eyebrows. "Plus, now I get a hot shifter of my own out of it."

Barking a rough laugh, Bailey shook his head. "Not sure who you're looking at—"

Pouncing, Clayton shoved Bailey to his back. He straddled his lover's waist while gripping his wrists. While he knew Bailey could have pulled away or moved him easily, his lover didn't.

Instead, Bailey smiled up indulgently at him.

"And I'm not sure who put ideas into your head that you're not hot, but I mean to replace it with the truth." Clayton leaned down and pecked a kiss to Bailey's lips. "You." He did it again and again, between each emphatic word. "Are. Hot." Then Clayton waggled his eyebrows. "And now, you're mine."

Bailey pulled free of Clayton's grip only to wrap his arms around him, holding him tightly to him. "Yes, I am."

Sliding one hand up, Bailey threaded his fingers into Clayton's hair and brought him down for a toe-curling kiss. As he mapped Clayton's mouth, suckling lightly on his tongue, he rolled them. In the next instant, Bailey rested in the vee of Clayton's thighs, cradling his head in his hand as he continued to kiss his lips, breathing noisily through his nose instead of pulling away.

At the same time, Bailey began rocking his hips.

When Clayton felt his hard shaft slide against his own, he moaned into Bailey's mouth, realizing what he wanted. He planted his feet and rolled his hips, helping his lover find the right position. Seconds later, he groaned again upon feeling Bailey's thick shaft sink back into his body.

CHAPTER NINE

Bailey strolled through the small town festival, marveling at the variety of booths and goods that were offered. One section was a traditional farmer's market with produce and organic baked goods. The other section offered trinkets, jewelry, clothes, toys, and other baubles.

And I'm openly holding my mate's hand. Never thought the day would come when I could do that.

There were so many same-sex couples milling around the place or manning booths — that in the secluded town of Stone Ridge — it seemed like the most natural thing in the world.

If Bailey had been on the fence about staying there before, that fact would have cured his uncertainty.

"What do you think of the place?" Clayton asked, peering up at him with a grin. "Pretty sweet, huh?"

Nodding, Bailey silently agreed. "I don't remember the last time I went to a small town festival like this. Was it like this last year?"

That morning, after their second round of sex, they'd eaten a late breakfast together. Clayton had spotted a message on his phone from an unknown number. It had turned out to be Ronan, telling them to expect their parents at Declan's at four o'clock. They would share the news that Bailey had woken at that time. Ronan had also promised to bring over some clothes that he and Markus had gathered from the other shifters in the pack.

Clayton had suggested the festival as a distraction while waiting.

"This is a little bigger than last year," Clayton told him. "But not by much. This is Stone Ridge's festival welcoming spring, one of the highlights of their year." Grinning, he added, "Wait until you see what they do for Halloween and Christmas."

"They like holidays, huh?" Bailey commented.

"I think it just gives them something to celebrate," Ronan stated from Bailey's other side. When he'd dropped off the clothes and heard where they were going, he and his mate, had decided to join them. "Otherwise, what the hell else would they do?"

Markus bumped his arm into Ronan's. "Sometimes, you are so cynical, my mate." He shook his head, but his tone was filled with warmth, and his eyes danced with amusement.

Ronan slung his arm around Markus's waist. "Sorry, babe."

"Love you anyway," Ronan countered.

Pausing right there in the middle of the walkway, Ronan dipped his head and pressed a quick kiss to Markus's lips.

Bailey smiled and kept walking. He liked seeing Ronan so happy. When his brother had returned from war an injured veteran, he'd been angry and frustrated with the world. Buying a fixer-upper house and planting a garden had helped give him something to do every day, but it was easy to see that now Ronan actually had a purpose again—making Markus happy.

I figure that's how I am, too.

Squeezing Clayton's hand, Bailey asked, "What's your favorite thing to check out here?"

Clayton shrugged. "I bought a bunch of earrings last year, but that was just to take them apart for the wiring."

Bailey barked a laugh as he grinned. "I hope you didn't tell the vender that was what you planned."

Scoffing, Clayton shot a wounded look Bailey's way. "Of course not!"

"Good." Bailey winked at his lover. "And I think it's nice. You helped out a local merchant instead of ordering from some big box store."

Clayton nodded. "Exactly." Then he scowled and grumbled, "Don't know why Lark didn't see it that way. He was scandalized."

"Lark is a doctor, Clay," Bailey pointed out. "He was probably scandalized about the bomb-building, not the earrings."

Brightening, Clayton asked, "You think so?"

Bailey didn't know for sure, but if it made his mate feel better, he would hold to that idea. "Most likely."

"I'll have to ask him when I see him tonight," Clayton stated before pointing at a booth with a variety of dreamcatchers. "I've always wanted one of those. When I moved to the states, I read up on a lot of the Native American cultures. They're fascinating."

"Let's find one you like, then," Bailey urged, heading them in that direction.

Clayton had been perusing the options for a couple of minutes when Ronan and Markus caught up. Bailey greeted his brother with a nod before asking, "Has Declan come up with a plan for explaining my sudden vitality to Mom?"

Ronan smirked. "A wheelchair."

Groaning, Bailey rolled his eyes. "You can't be serious."

"Afraid so." Ronan patted him on the shoulder. "It'll only be for a couple of weeks and only around her. It's not like—"

"Ronan? Markus?"

The call of a female voice Bailey recognized caused tension to ratchet up his spine. He, Ronan, and Markus all turned to see his younger sister, Isabel, rushing toward them. She was accompanied by a brown-headed man Bailey didn't recognize.

A quick glance around revealed his parents weren't in sight, but that didn't mean they weren't there somewhere.

Shit. Why didn't I think of that?

"Isabel. Hey," Ronan greeted, stepping in front of Bailey, shielding him from view. As Ronan moved to embrace Isabel, Markus took a position to hide him. "Didn't realize you'd be interested in coming here, Sis, or I woulda invited you," Ronan continued. "Mom and Dad with you?"

Isabel sighed deeply. "No, Mom's on another kick about your *lifestyle*," she told them, sounding frustrated. "And Dad's trying to reason with her. I had to get out of there or I woulda screamed."

That was good, at least.

"Hey, Daithi," Markus greeted the dark-haired man. "I didn't realize you knew Isabel."

"I didn't," Daithi replied. "But I was visitin' Reb at his tattoo parlor, and Dixon and Helsinki were there. Dixon recognized her." He chuckled as he said, "Poor Hels hates needles, but he'll do anythin' for Dixon. He's getting' his nipples pierced."

As Bailey physically cringed, Ronan hissed. "Ouch."

"Aye, agreed," Daithi continued. "Anyway, he didna think ye'd appreciate Isabel wanderin' the town by herself." He cleared his throat and finished, "No' until certain . . . issues are resolved."

"I agree, and thank you," Ronan replied.

Isabel sighed. "I would have been fine."

Ronan's voice turned brotherly. "I sure hope so, Bel, but better safe than sorry." Then he cleared his throat and asked, "Can you keep a secret?"

Bailey's heart began to race in his chest, wondering if Ronan was about to do what he suspected. He desperately wanted to yank his sister into a hug, but he feared her response. Blood was beginning to rush in his ears, making it difficult to eavesdrop on the conversation.

Then Bailey felt Clayton's hand slip back into his own. He blinked open eyes he didn't remember closing and met his lover's gaze. With a smile of thanks, he pulled Clayton into his arms, careful not to crush the bag his mate held.

"You know I can, but are you sure *you* should tell," Isabel teased.

"You would have found out this afternoon anyway," Ronan told her. "Let's head off to the side."

Out of the corner of his eye, Bailey spotted Ronan leading Isabel and Daithi through the crowd. Behind her back, Ronan held up his hand, fingers spread, indicating to give them five minutes.

Bailey nodded.

"Where are they going?" Bailey asked Markus after they were out of earshot.

"To get a funnel cake," Markus told him. "We'll follow in a few, after he gets the particulars out of the way."

Bailey licked his lips and hummed. "Funnel cake." His cat purred in his mind, particularly interested in the whipped cream.

Clayton chuckled softly. "Like the sound of that, huh?"

"Can't remember the last time I had one," Bailey admitted. Sobering, he added, "And I really want to see my sister."

"She'll be overjoyed to see you, too," Markus assured. "No matter what."

Bailey nodded, praying the other shifter was right. Clearing his throat, he focused on Clayton. "Find the one you want?"

Nodding, Clayton smiled up at him. "It'll look great with the colors in our bedroom."

Our bedroom.

Grinning, Bailey stated, "I can't wait to see it."

"Let's mosey toward the food vendors," Markus offered. "We'll scope out where they're at, and I can check to see if it's okay for you to approach."

Bailey blew out a breath, uncertain why he felt so nervous. Slipping his hand in Clayton's, he followed Markus through the crowds. He appreciated his lover's light squeeze of encouragement.

They reached the food vendor section and eating tents, and the butterflies in Bailey's gut intensified. If he felt this nervous about seeing his sister, he wondered how bad the meeting with his parents would be. He couldn't figure out why he wasn't excited, instead.

Between other patrons, Bailey spotted Isabel and Ronan sitting off to the side. There were tears on her cheeks, but her expression appeared happy, hopeful. When Ronan pulled one of his hands free and pointed in Bailey's direction, Isabel's attention immediately swept the crowd for him.

As soon as their gazes locked, all Bailey's nerves dissipated. The look of absolute joy on his sister's face cleared them all away. She jumped to her feet and sprinted toward him, nearly knocking over several people in her haste, not that she seemed to notice.

Bailey opened his arms and braced. Isabel slammed full steam against him, and he suddenly appreciated his increased shifter strength. He wrapped her in a tight yet careful hug, lifting her off her feet and swinging her around.

"Bai-Bai!" Isabel screamed in Bailey's ear, and he did his best not to wince. "You're here. You're really here!"

After a few seconds where Bailey knew they were making a complete spectacle, he felt Ronan's hand on his shoulder. He settled Isabel back on her feet and grinned down at her. "Yeah, I'm here," he murmured, keeping one arm around her as he turned her to walk together. "It's so damn good to see you."

Ronan guided them both back toward the food tables, where Daithi was watching from a distance.

Clayton touched Bailey's upper arm and softly told him, "I'll get us some funnel cakes. Blueberries?"

Bailey paused and cradled Clayton's jaw with his free

hand. "Thanks, Clay." Then he dipped his head and pecked a quick kiss to his lover's lips before whispering, "Strawberries, if they have it."

Beaming up at him, Clayton murmured, "I'll look." Then his mate headed toward the food trucks.

Spotting Markus following Clayton, Bailey appreciated the other shifter's instincts. He needed his mate protected, but he needed a minute with his family, too. The wolf shifter respected that.

Turning his attention back to his siblings, Bailey spotted Isabel's wide-eyed expression, and he noticed the spicy scent of shock.

Huh. I'm getting the hang of this scenting stuff.

Although he couldn't say how he knew . . . just that he did.

Lifting his lips into a half-smile, Bailey murmured, "Surprise."

"You're gay, too?" Isabel snickered, her hazel eyes twinkling with mirth. "Oh, Mom is gonna shit purple kittens. All her kids are gay!"

"Watch your mouth," Ronan commented, although it sounded more like rote. Then his brows shot up. "You're gay, too?"

Isabel nibbled her bottom lip as she nodded, glancing between them. "Is that okay?"

Ronan rolled his eyes as Bailey guided Isabel to a chair. "Of course it is." After she sat, he pulled a chair close to hers and settled next to her. "Why would you even ask us that?" Bailey didn't bother correcting her misconception about him being gay, since he would forever be with Clayton, a man.

Their brother sat on the other side, and Daithi relaxed a few chairs down with chili cheese fries that smelled amazing.

"Ronan said you woke up yesterday?"

Ignoring his stomach, Bailey focused back on Isabel. He lifted his hand in a so-so gesture. "I woke up once and panicked, and Lark gave me a sedative. I don't know how long ago that was." Seeing her expressive eyes filled with concern, Bailey quickly assured, "I'm fine now. Really."

"I didn't realize that," Ronan cut in. "Lark didn't mention anything."

Bailey shrugged. "He probably doesn't think I remember." Then he focused on Isabel again. "I didn't know where I was, and I didn't remember who I was, so I ran." He left out that he'd shifted into a cheetah. It wasn't the place to share that detail. "I found a cave to hide out in. I thought it was secluded and a good place to think." Chuckling softly, Bailey swept his gaze over the crowd until he spotted Clayton, who was standing in a line with Markus. "Imagine my surprise when my mate wanders into the cave for a picnic."

"Your mate?" Isabel latched onto that. "Does that mean . . ." She followed his line of sight, glancing at Clayton, before refocusing on him. "Does that mean you can" — she waved her hand in the air — "you know?"

Nodding once more, Bailey was beginning to feel like a bobblehead. "Yes to the *you know*," he stated with a smile.

"Then why did you run from them?" Isabel appeared confused.

Bailey rubbed at his temple and admitted, "I had no memory of who I was. I only knew my name because Lark called me that." Frowning, Bailey lowered his voice and told her, "It took a little time and an information dump from Castrose, that's Clayton's brother, for everything to come crashing back." He scoffed as he added, "Then I passed out again. Not my finest moment."

"Oh, no," Ronan countered with a smirk. "Not your finest moment is when you were carried by Castrose back to the house when you were buck-ass nude."

"Language," Isabel teased even as she snickered. "Naked, huh?" Then she cocked her head, considering. "That makes sense." Pointing discreetly at an approaching Clayton, Isabel murmured, "So, Clayton is your mate?"

Bailey couldn't help but grin as he watched Clayton's approach. "Oh, yeah."

Not only did the slender blond juggle two fried bread, one with strawberries and a second with blueberries, but he also held a water bottle under that arm. In his other hand, he carried a massive plate of chili cheese fries. A second bottle of water was under that arm.

Clayton concentrated so hard, his tongue sticking out to touch the corner of his top lip, he didn't even notice their perusal.

"Oh, you have it so bad," Isabel teased, grinning.

Sighing, Bailey knew he sported a goofy smile when both his siblings chuckled. "Yeah. Yeah, I do."

Isabel patted his arm. "Well, I'm happy for you."

"Thank you." Bailey squeezed his sister's shoulder, appreciating her support.

"So, what are you going to tell Mom and Dad?" Isabel asked. "I'll go along with whatever, so just let me know."

Then Clayton arrived, placing the food before them all. "I saw you eyeing Daithi's fries," he revealed with a laugh.

"Thank you, cute Clay." Bailey pulled him down into the seat on his free side, feeling damn grateful for the man Fate had given him. "Meet my sister, Isabel."

CHAPTER TEN

"Try to relax," Clayton urged, rubbing over Bailey's shirt-covered shoulder. "It doesn't matter what she says, remember? I'm not going anywhere."

Bailey inhaled deeply, his eyes closing. Then he let out the breath before staring up at him again. Gratefulness filled his brown eyes.

"Thank you." Bailey grimaced. "I know it's really supposed to be me reassuring you because it's my mother, but damn if this need to grab you and run fast isn't driving me nuts."

Clayton chuckled as he rubbed Bailey's shoulder again. "It's fine." With a wink, he added, "Like you."

As usual, Bailey rolled his eyes as if he didn't believe him. *Oh well. Someday.*

Bailey did reach up and rest a hand over Clayton's own. His shifter sat in the wheelchair provided by Lark. He wore dark-blue sweatpants, a light-blue shirt, and white socks.

The plan was for Lark to text Clayton as soon as it was time for him to take him to the study to be reunited with his parents.

"I hear a vehicle," Bailey murmured, cocking his head. He scoffed softly. "Their suburban still sounds the same."

Clayton frowned. "Someone could use that to track them." Shaking his head, he claimed, "They need a new vehicle."

Bailey stared at him in surprise. "You're right."

"Don't act so surprised." Clayton smirked and winked, softening his admonishment. "I told you I have survival training."

Grinning, Bailey murmured, "Yes, you did."

"I don't care if Ronan is paying for this private clinic," a woman yelled so loud even Clayton's human hearing didn't have any trouble understanding her. "You cannot keep me from my son."

Huh. So that's how they decided to play it for her new memory. Clayton had wondered.

Several masculine voices rumbled together, and Clayton didn't understand them.

Bailey must have, however. He grimaced and stated, "We better go sooner rather than later. She's threatening to call the cops."

Snorting, Clayton took his mate at his word. "A fat lot of good it would do her," he told him as he began wheeling him out of the bedroom. He turned to the right, the back of the house, and the elevator. "The pack practically owns the cops."

"They do?"

"Mmm-hmmm," Clayton confirmed. "Declan leaked information about Sheriff Parkinson, stuff revealing him to be a homophobe."

"Damn. I bet that didn't go over well around here."

Clayton grinned. "Nope. He was removed from office last week. Right now, Detective Grady Stryker is the acting sheriff. He's a Bengal tiger shifter, but he doesn't want the job. Alpha Declan is looking for a suitable replacement."

"How do you know all this?" Curiosity filled Bailey's voice as he leaned forward and pushed the *down* button. "I thought you spent most of your time in your shop."

"I used to live with Dixon."

A low growl erupted from Bailey, and Clayton snickered while wheeling them into the elevator.

"In the guest room," Clayton clarified, silently loving Bailey's possessive display. "So I've always pretty much had the run of the place. Although, I'm much more careful about my comings and goings now that Dixon is mated."

Bailey curled his lip as he scowled up at Clayton. "You lived with him *before* he was mated?"

Rolling his eyes, Clayton slapped his shoulder lightly with the back of his hand. "Nothing happened. Control yourself," he ordered even as he chuckled. "So, anyway." Clayton punched the button for the first floor and started them moving. "I slipped into his place for a piece of this cake that Helsinki made." Remembering the rich, German chocolate cake, he hummed. "So good."

It was Bailey's turn to chuckle. He squeezed Clayton's hand. "Focus. Maybe we'll get you cake on the way home."

Grinning, Clayton nodded. "So, I'm in the kitchen pulling out a paper plate when I hear low murmurs." His cheeks heated as he admitted to sneaking down the hall to Dixon's study. "Alpha Declan was telling Dixon about Sheriff Parkinson's removal and how they needed to find a replacement. They were tossing out names." Lowering his voice, Clayton continued, "Some look on Dixon's face must have tipped Declan off because the alpha asked what he was thinking about.

"Dixon sounded pained when he answered, telling that he might have a good candidate." Clayton warmed to his gossiping as he began pushing the chair out of the elevator. "Then Dixon told Declan about his semi-estranged brother. He wasn't quite as dominant as Dixon, but they still butted heads quite a bit. They hadn't been in the same pack for over a hundred years because of it."

"Why would Dixon think that was a good fit?" Bailey asked in confusion.

Clayton shrugged. "Said that his brother was always there if he needed him and that he was a good man."

Bailey shook his head. "How would he be a good fit if he couldn't follow the beta?"

"I don't know," Clayton admitted. "I —"

"So we *did* hear you eavesdropping on pack business that day."

Clayton spun and winced, spotting Dixon behind them. The big beta's ice-blue eyes were narrowed, and he had his arms crossed over his brawny chest. The corner of his mouth was curved in a disapproving expression.

"U-Um, sorry?" Clayton squeaked.

Scoffing, Dixon rolled his eyes and relaxed. "Yeah. Right." He headed toward them. "I was hoping to catch you in the room and tell you to stay there, but you left early." Smirking, Dixon stared down at Clayton, a twinkle entering his eyes. "I took the back stairs to catch up with you. Funny what you can find out when you eavesdrop."

Rubbing the back of his neck, Clayton smiled sheepishly at the beta. "I came for cake but heard you talking. I was curious."

Dixon gripped the back of Clayton's neck and squeezed lightly. "It's fine," he stated softly with a shake of his head. "It's pack business anyway, so everyone will know what we've decided eventually."

"Are you really inviting your brother here?" Clayton asked curiously. "What's his name? Is he a wolf, too?" He knew better than to assume, even amidst family members. "Will he defer to Declan even if he has trouble deferring to you?"

As his countenance morphed into a longsuffering expression, Dixon used his hold to start Clayton forward. "You heard an awful lot." He released him and grabbed the handles of Bailey's wheelchair. "You'll have to wait, just like everyone else."

Clayton pouted for an instant. Then a woman asking loudly, "Where is he?" caused him to wince.

"Wow. She's got a set of lungs on her," Dixon grumbled.

"Never realized she could yell so loud," Bailey muttered,

rubbing his ear.

"With your increased hearing, it'll only get worse the closer she gets," Dixon told him with a grimace. "Clayton, open the office door."

Hustling forward, Clayton quickly obeyed. He swung the door wide and led the way into the expansive room. Half of it contained a large desk with a couple of comfortable-looking chairs before it. There was a bench against the wall for extra seating, along with a couple of bookshelves. The other side had been set up like a relaxed sitting area with a sideboard, several leather chairs and small sofas, end tables, and a coffee table.

Dixon went to the right and positioned Bailey beside a chair. Clayton immediately sat and took his lover's hand. To his relief, Bailey didn't hesitate in the move and even rubbed his thumb over the back of his own.

"What do you want to drink?" Dixon asked, heading to the sideboard. "I'd recommend whiskey to deal with your mother, but I suppose that would look funny considering you're supposed to be on meds."

Bailey shook his head. "I wouldn't want anything to compromise my judgment right now anyhow. What about some orange juice?"

Bending, Dixon pulled a single-serve bottle from the minifridge under the side board. "I guess no one told you, yet." He crossed to Bailey and held it out. Smirking, he added, "With your increased metabolism, it'd take quite a bit of alcohol to affect you."

"Can't get drunk?" Bailey asked as he took the bottle, his brows lifting a bit.

Dixon shrugged. "You can, but it takes considerable hard liquor."

Bailey chuckled as he unscrewed the lid. "I'll remember that but probably won't test it out anytime soon."

Nodding, Dixon turned his attention to Clayton. "For you?"

After a second of hesitation, Clayton asked, "Do you have white wine?"

"Sure do."

Dixon returned to the sideboard. He pulled out a bottle and popped the cork. While Dixon was placing a wine glass on the wooden surface, a small, grandmotherly-looking woman rushed into the room.

"Bai-Bai!" she screeched, freezing for a heartbeat. She had her hands clutched to her ample bosom, and her pale blue eyes teared up behind her glasses. "Oh, my dear Bai-Bai. Is that you?"

"Hi, Ma," Bailey greeted with a smile. "It's so good to see you."

As if hearing Bailey speak unlocked some sort of dam, Victoria — Bailey had told Clayton his parents' names earlier that day, and his father was Greg — rushed across the room. She settled in the chair on Bailey's other side and reached for his hand . . . which contained the juice. Taking it, she set it on the side table before wrapping Bailey's hand between both of her own.

"How are you, Bai-Bai?" Victoria crooned. "Are you sure you're okay to be up? Are you pushing yourself?" She swept her gaze over Bailey with a critical eye. "I can take you back to bed, or better yet, I could take you to the house we're renting. I'll make certain everything is taken care of."

Without missing a beat, or giving Bailey a chance to counter her, Victoria looked over her shoulder at Greg, who still stood in the doorway with shock on his face. "Greg, honey, come see Bailey."

Greg shook himself out of his stupor and hurried into the room. The older man glanced from Bailey to Clayton to their clasped hands back to Clayton and finally returning to Bailey.

Except, he didn't say anything.

Maybe Isabel had told him.

They'd left the festival with Isabel promising to act surprised, but so far, she was hanging back.

Had something changed?

Grabbing the coffee table, Greg positioned it a couple of feet in front of Bailey's chair. "Hell, son. How are you feeling?"

Bailey smiled at his father. "It's good to be up and around," he told the aging man. "Thanks for coming here."

Greg smiled warmly. "Nowhere else we'd rather be."

"Do you have a bag, sweetie?" Victoria asked. Turning in her seat, she eyed Lark. "Surely he can come with us, and that's why he's in the wheelchair. Recovery at home is so much more comfortable than in a clinic." Her eyes narrowed as she glanced between Lark and Declan, the alpha having his arm slung possessively around his mate's waist. "No matter how nice."

Bailey released Clayton long enough to pat Victoria's hand, which held his other one. Then he reached down and picked up his juice. He handed it to Clayton, asking, "Will you open that for me, please?"

Clayton silently appreciated Bailey's attempt to ease him into the conversation.

As Clayton opened the juice, Bailey held his free hand out to Isabel. "I'm not fragile, Isabel. Come give your brother a hug."

On a gasp that could easily be mistaken for a sob, Isabel ran forward. Even as Victoria warned her to be careful, she threw her arms around him and gave him a tight hug. The move also allowed Bailey to pull free of Victoria so he could wrap his sister in a hug.

After several seconds, Victoria gripped Isabel's upper arm, saying, "Don't crush him, darling. He's recovering."

Isabel released Bailey and straightened. Then she found a seat on the nearest sofa, curling her legs under herself and leaning over the arm to remain as close as possible. Ronan sat down beside her, and Markus leaned against the arm.

"Here," Clayton offered, holding out the drink.

Bailey murmured his thanks and took a deep swallow. After handing it back, his mother snagged his hand again.

Clayton set the juice aside, finding a glass of white wine there, too. Casting a grateful glance toward Dixon, he found the alpha, alpha-mate, and beta halfway across the room. He figured they were trying to be supportive without being intrusive. He noticed Castrose and Eion had shown up at some point, too.

Tucking his left leg under his butt, Clayton got comfortable, leaning toward Bailey in his wheelchair. He rested his left hand on the arm with the wine glass on his thigh with his right. Tuning back into the conversation, he heard Bailey counter his mother.

"I really appreciate the offer, Mom," Bailey began. "And I know it comes from a place of love, but I already have a place to stay."

"I thought you just woke up," Victoria stated, her full lips in a bit of a pout. "Do you plan to stay with Ronan?" Her expression turned a little accusatory as she glanced at the pair before refocusing on Bailey and smiling brightly again. "Because I don't think that will work. I've been there. The bedrooms are upstairs."

Damn. Didn't think of that.

Clayton took a sip of his wine to hide his grimace. He knew if she discovered his own place was on the second floor, she would try to use the same argument. Clayton wondered if it would be too much to ask that she would be so outraged about them being together that she wouldn't visit for a few months.

"No, not at Ronan's," Bailey told his mother. With a small

smile, he stated, "I knew you were never a fan when Ronan came out as gay, so I never said anything about my own interest in men." Her eyes widened the more Bailey spoke. Clayton felt his heart melt when Bailey took his hand and flashed him a warm smile before refocusing on his mother. "I'd like to introduce you to Clayton Zukan. I asked Ronan to track him down last night, as soon as I could speak." With a fake hitch in his voice, Bailey whispered, "And even after me being gone all this time, he came." He focused on Clayton again. "I'll never hide you again, baby. Thank you for giving me another chance."

After swallowing the sudden lump in his throat—even knowing it was acting—Clayton whispered, "You're my soul mate." He did his best to give his sexy military lover a tough stare. "And hell no, you won't, or we're going to have words."

"Sorry." Bailey grimaced, appearing chagrined.

That hadn't been the plan, as he'd been trying to be funny. "No more apologies," he whispered. Neither one of them owed each other those words.

Rearing back, releasing his hand in the process, Victoria cried, "You can't be serious." She glanced between them with distaste, shaking her head as if that would make it all go away. Then Victoria glared at Ronan. "Is this your doing? Did you encourage this deviant behavior?"

Ronan narrowed his eyes as he claimed, "No, I didn't know." His lips tightened as he continued, "But even if I had, I would have told Bailey to follow his heart, no matter where it led."

Victoria jumped to her feet. "But this is wrong." She pointed at where Ronan had his arm around Markus's waist. "And you were supposed to grow out of it."

Bailey heaved a deep sigh and shook his head. "That attitude's why I never told you, Mom."

CHAPTER ELEVEN

"Well, that went about as well as I thought it would." Ronan slouched back on the love seat, a beer in hand. He had his arm wrapped around Markus's waist and held his mate to his side.

Bailey groaned and shook his head from his own position on the love seat. He'd moved beside Clayton as soon as his mother had left. While what he'd said was true—he'd always known his mother wasn't accepting of gays and thought Ronan would grow out of that phase—never would he have thought she would threaten to cut them from her life. After all, his parents had always touted a motto about *anything for our children.*

Sure, Bailey and Ronan had been away a lot, doing missions in the military, for a couple of decades, but he wondered when her mentality had changed.

Five minutes ago, Victoria had stormed from the house, herding an angry Isabel before her. She'd threatened to never let them see their sister again if they didn't denounce their deviant ways. Their father had lingered a moment, assuring them that he wouldn't allow that to happen before following his wife and daughter.

"I feel the worst for Isabel," Bailey told everyone. "She's the one stuck in the house with our angry mother." Frowning, he focused on Ronan. "You lived in their neck of the woods for three years before I disappeared. Did you see any of this coming?"

"This?" Ronan arched one brow. "This, as in meeting a

man who introduced me to the paranormal world and turned my world on its head?"

Snorting a laugh, Bailey smirked at his brother. Leave it to Ronan to find some way to make him laugh in a stressful situation. He gratefully took the glass of vodka from Dixon. At some point, Helsinki had joined them, and he looked distinctly uncomfortable where he sat on the sofa. For an instant, Bailey wondered why.

Then Dixon crossed to him and helped him gently remove his polo shirt. The silver hoops in his freshly pierced nipples gleamed in the lights of the study. Dixon picked up a cloth napkin and held it out to Helsinki, saying, "I'm sorry it hurts, baby."

Helsinki took the napkin and opened it. A relieved expression crossed the big man's face, and he pulled out a couple of ice cubes. After setting the remaining bundle aside, Helsinki relaxed back on the love seat and lifted the cubes to his freshly pierced nipples.

Clayton met Bailey's gaze with a serious expression. "No," he stated firmly. "Never going to happen."

Bailey did his best to hold in a laugh, although he couldn't help the way the corners of his lips twitched. "Maybe in a few years we—"

"No." Clayton frowned at him. "Just no."

Chuckling, Bailey grabbed Clayton and tugged him close. "Okay."

"How did you convince Hels to pierce his nipples?" Lark asked curiously, cocking his head.

Helsinki scowled at Dixon. "He said it would only hurt for a little while." His expression turned petulant. "It's been *hours.*"

Bailey wanted to laugh at the huge man who appeared ready to whimper piteously.

Dixon settled next to Helsinki and rested his hand on Helsinki's thigh. "I'm sorry, babe. So very sorry." His expression betrayed his upset as he admitted, "I thought I'd be able to take you straight home afterward. If I saturate your nipples in my saliva, it'll heal them almost immediately." He lifted his hand to touch Helsinki's neck. "Just like when we claim each other." Staring earnestly at his mate, the beta appeared so very apologetic. "But we were delayed, and pack business got in the way, and we had to come straight here and—"

Helsinki touched an ice cube to Dixon's lips, stalling his verbal diarrhea. "It's okay," he replied with a small smile, returning the cube to his nipple. "I'll be okay. I'm just bein' a big baby."

Growling softly, Dixon's blue eyes seemed to glow with need. "You're my baby, Hels. Never forget that."

While Bailey had never imagined he would see the big, dominant wolf upset and uncertain, seeing him aroused and needy—the scent of his desire flooding the air—was even more unimaginable. His gut twisted as a thought hit him. These guys acted just like his team when they got together to blow off steam.

Bailey frowned as he lowered his gaze to the floor.

Where are they now?

"Hey. You okay?" Clayton murmured, rubbing his thigh. "We'll figure this out with your family."

Smiling wanly at Clayton, Bailey admitted, "I was actually thinking that everyone's bantering reminded me of the guys. I'm just wondering where they ended up."

"I have a lead!"

Bailey snapped his head around and spotted Prier sauntering into the room. He was followed by his mate, Kajika, as well as another male—a redhead who smelled to be human.

Castrose tipped his head to the side a little as he eyed the newcomers. "Do you loiter about in the halls, waiting for the perfect time to make a grand entrance?" he asked while tapping his trigger finger on the beer bottle he held.

For some reason, Bailey got the distinct impression that his new brother-in-law — a sniper by trade — was imagining shooting the human.

As if Prier was thinking the same thing, he lifted his thumb and forefinger in the image of a gun and made a cocking noise. "Of course not." Lowering his hand, he winked. "I'm just that good." Prier grinned broadly as he set down his laptop case on the coffee table and began pulling out the machine. Grinning at Castrose, he added, "Oh, and I have listening devices in key positions of meeting rooms. I'm in hiding, after all, and can't have every Tom, Dick, and Harry seeing my face."

Castrose did not look impressed. "Really?"

"He had permission," Alpha Declan cut in, ending the conversation. Returning his attention to Prier, he asked, "What do you and Raul have?"

"I researched all General Sacketts and Doctor Winoans and found a money trail to a company called Winter Heights Pharmaceuticals."

Bailey wondered if there was something significant to that that he just wasn't getting because he was the new guy, but everyone else seemed to be waiting for the punch line, too.

Raul seemed to be the less dramatic one, for he quickly picked up the explanation. "Winter Heights Pharmaceuticals boasts being on the cutting edge of life-extension drugs and anti-aging serums." The corners of the redhead's lips tightened. "They've also been picketed by animal activist groups on at least six occasions over the last ten years." Shaking his head, Raul told everyone, "They always seem to squeak by inspections without any problems. The reviewer indicates in his or her notes that there are cages, but they're always empty. Except, infiltrators provide pictures with those same cages full of animals."

"So, they're really good at hiding where they smuggle their animals to?" Dixon guessed.

Bailey felt his gut clench. "Or those animals are shifters, and the scientists can control what form they're in." Focusing on Raul, who seemed the less combative of the pair, he asked, "Are there security barracks on the premises? That would be a perfect place to hide an unconscious shifter in human form."

Raul tapped at his computer as Prier smirked at Bailey. "I like the way he thinks." Chuckling coldly, he mused, "What inspector would think to ask the guards to wake up those who were supposed to be *off shift*." Prier lifted his fingers in air quotes.

Appreciating that his idea was being taken seriously, Bailey nodded. "Exactly."

"Are we going to infiltrate one of their facilities?" Clayton asked curiously before taking a sip of his wine.

"Sounds like fun," Prier commented.

"Well, it won't be you," Kajika countered, resting a hand on Prier's shoulder. "We're in hiding. Remember?"

Prier sighed deeply. "Yes, Injun."

"Then who?" Dixon asked, sweeping his gaze around the room. "Who in the pack could pass for a scientist and whose face isn't known by some agency?"

Everyone seemed to either be exchanging looks or be deep in thought.

Bailey saw Clayton slowly lift his hand, and he really didn't like the firm look on his face.

Declan licked his lips as he glanced between them. "This may be something ye want to discuss with yer mate first, Clayton."

"No." Not surprisingly, Castrose spoke up before Bailey did. "You're not going undercover."

As much as Bailey wanted to back up Castrose one hundred percent, his shifter nature wanted to support Clayton, too. Of course, Bailey's instincts also screamed at him to keep Clayton safe.

"Is there a way I can go with him?" Bailey asked softly.

"No!" Castrose repeated on a growl.

Eion threaded their fingers together and squeezed lightly. "Take a deep breath, my mate. We would never purposefully put your brother in harms' way." He managed to pull Castrose's focus away from Clayton. "If anyone goes in, there will be many back-up contingencies."

Castrose's nostrils flared, but he didn't counter his mate. Instead, he cut a hard look Clayton's way.

Clayton smiled calmly at Castrose. "I remember how shocked these guys were when they walked into our basement hideout and found me there." He chuckled softly as he obviously recalled the memory. "They were expecting you and didn't have a clue I existed."

"According to our records," Raul cut in. "You died at fifteen in a house fire."

Nodding, Clayton confirmed, "We worked very hard to dot all our *I*s and cross all our *T*s for that story." He continued to hold his brother's stare. "No one knows I exist, and we'll keep it that way. You know the Romanians thought it was you hiding there."

"But they know I work with someone," Castrose countered.

Grinning, Clayton countered, "But not a skinny, geeky little brother."

"You're not skinny or geeky," Bailey snapped, unable to keep his mouth shut.

Clayton smiled at Bailey. "And you don't think you're a sexy soldier." With a shrug, he added, "We are always our own worst critic. Right?"

Understanding, Bailey nodded. "Right." Then he sobered, saying, "I just found you. There's no way I want to lose you just as quickly."

"You won't."

Clayton sounded so certain that Bailey didn't have the heart to stop his mate. Instead, he nuzzled into his lover's palm and tried to control the fear that threatened to permeate his system. One way or another, Bailey would figure out a way to back him up.

"I have an idea that you're really going to hate," Raul offered slowly, still tapping away at his computer.

Alpha Declan groaned, rubbing his palm over his face. "Let's hear it."

Raul tore his gaze away from his computer and glanced around the group. After licking his lips, the man offered, "Well, I don't see a way for Clayton to go into a pharmaceutical company with a guard, however" — he straightened in his seat and rubbed his thighs — "he could be going to collaborate on a serum . . . and he would take his *project* with him."

Declan sucked in a harsh breath, his deep gray eyes narrowing. "Are ye suggestin' we knock Bailey out and having Clayton take him with him as a . . . a *project*?"

"Yes," Raul replied simply. Lifting his hands, palms out in placation, he hurried to ask Clayton, "How many languages do you speak?"

Clayton seemed surprised by the question, but he answered readily enough. "Six fluently, and I'm okay in another five." Wagging his head a little, Clayton looked to be doing some mental calculations before adding, "I can normally get by in another four."

Raul nodded. "I guessed as much."

"Why?" Bailey blurted, unable to help himself.

Shrugging, Raul stated, "He doesn't have even a hint of an accent."

Grinning broadly, Clayton quipped, "Thanks, but I can sound southern or like I'm from the Bronx if you need me to."

Chuckling softly, Raul shook his head. "Not necessary. How's your Russian?"

Clayton shrugged. "Fluent."

"That is brilliant, my friend." Prier pointed at something on Raul's computer over his shoulder. "One of the places we blew up five years ago?"

Raul nodded. "We can pass him off as a scientist who fled and went underground for years until the heat died down." Grinning coldly, he sneered. "We'll add a couple of shady sales to his identity. Maybe a failed genetic experiment, as well as some successful trials for healing humans using shifter DNA. If Edwin can give us some mock trials, they'll jump at the chance to collaborate."

Bailey realized just how fast these guys planned, making him feel like he was being thrust behind enemy lines with only half the necessary information. Still, he would never refuse a mission and leave any of his people short-handed or in jeopardy. The same was happening now, and he turned to peer at Ronan . . . only to find his brother staring right back at him.

Reading the look in Ronan's eyes — *I just got you back, don't go dying on me* — Bailey smiled tightly. Then he returned his focus back to the discussion.

He would talk with his brother in private before anything went down, but some sixth sense he always trusted told him he needed to be on his A-game for this one.

Lifting his hand as if he were a kid in school, Bailey called, "Question." Everyone paused to stare at him. Clearing his throat, Bailey asked, "How can we know that Doctor Winoan may be there?"

One way or another, Bailey would find a way to convince Clayton to stay home if they couldn't confirm that shifters were being experimented on ahead of time.

"Don't worry," Prier assured. "It's going to take a few days to put together a proper identity and backtrail for Clayton. During that time, we will narrow down which facility is our best bet to find your friends."

Bailey nodded even as he countered, "They're not my only concern."

Prier met his gaze squarely. "But they are your top concern."

Sighing, Bailey nodded. "Yes, they are."

Dixon wiggled his finger to point between him and Clayton. "Before you go in, you make certain you know exactly who you're going to choose if you can only take one of them out of that facility."

His gut clenching at the insinuation, Bailey growled low in his throat. "I know who I'll choose."

CHAPTER TWELVE

This is a really, really stupid idea. Why did I agree to this? What the hell was I thinking?

Even as Clayton mentally berated himself for his cocky attitude, he scowled at the loading dock workers and yelled, "Hey! You be careful there. That specimen is worth more than ten years of your salary."

Calling Bailey in animal form a specimen almost caused bile to rise in the back of his throat.

Still, Clayton's attitude garnered a reaction from the dock workers, and they used more care while unloading Bailey's crate. He'd already shared three calls with Doctor Nerian, one of the head researchers, and had managed to make a good impression. Every time Clayton struggled with a concept, he responded half in Russian and English, allowing him to blame it on linguistic differences.

Then he would talk to Edwin—a former CIA scientist—as well as Drake and Lark, so he would know how to respond properly in the future.

"Doctor Kuzmich?"

Clayton turned to face the female speaker, keeping a haughty expression on his face. "Dah?"

The woman smiled and held out her hand. "I'm Lorian, special aid to Doctor Nerian." After he'd shaken her hand, knowing that was actually a fancy way of saying she was his top nurse in experiments, Lorian indicated a door. "If you'll come with me, I'll show you to the doctor."

"And my animal?" Clayton glanced toward the unconscious Bailey. "It will be well taken care of?"

Clayton couldn't help but double-check. He knew Lark's serum would render Bailey asleep for six hours total. It had already been one. In the lining of his coat was a counteragent, just in case Clayton needed his lover to wake up sooner.

Unfortunately, he needed to be able to get to Bailey within the huge facility to use it.

"Of course," Lorian replied quickly. "Our specimens are handled with the utmost care." Her smile appeared bright and sunny. If she had any idea that the animals were actually sentient, she didn't care. "They are our company's life-blood, after all."

Well, that sounds like a company line if I've ever heard one.

Dipping his chin, Clayton turned to head toward the door Lorian had indicated. "Indeed."

Lorian used a key card to open the door and held it open for him. Dutifully, he passed through, even though his skin crawled at having to leave Bailey behind. The hairs on his nape stood on end, but he did his best to ignore it.

At least no one searched me.

If a guard had, they would have found his tranquilizer gun but not the pistol in a discreet holster hidden under his fake bit of belly flab. Even the knife in his left shoe would have been missed.

"So, how long have you been working with gene therapy?" Lorian asked with a smile.

Considering Lorian had been in on Nerian's calls, Clayton didn't see the need for the small talk. He wondered if she was trying to trip him up. Was this a test?

"Fourteen years," Clayton replied.

Lorian swept her gaze over his slender frame. "Oh, my. You must have started young." Cocking her head, she pressed, "Were you a prodigy?"

Clayton offered her a tight smile. "In Russia, we discover

our passions young and are encourage to pursue them to the exclusion of other things."

"Oh." Lorian nodded as if his comment made perfect sense.

It wasn't really true, but whatever.

Lorian opened her mouth, probably to ask another prying question, so Clayton cut her off at the pass. "This place is quite impressive. Have you worked here long?"

Fortunately, that sent Lorian on a tangent that told Clayton not only all about Lorian's career path, but also about the facility itself. She confirmed that there were three stories and fifteen labs. However, she also admitted to eight *projects* currently *in house.*

Damn.

Clayton vowed to find a way to tap out a message to the currently-listening Raul and Prier. They'd confirmed that they knew Morse code, and so did he. Also inside his fake fat, they'd installed a microphone and a button to pass on messages.

Pausing in the middle of the hall, Clayton placed his hand over his stomach and made a face.

"Are you okay?" Lorian asked, just as he'd assumed she would.

Twisting his lips into an uncomfortable expression, Clayton told her, "I have trouble with first meetings, which is why I like modern technology." He glanced up and down the hall. "May I visit the men's room before meeting Nerian?"

Lorian's eyes widened, and she quickly nodded. "Of course. This way." As she hurried forward, she added, "Nerian is really a fantastic scientist. There really is nothing to be worried about."

"I surmised as much." Clayton gave her a beseeching smile. "Sometimes, nerves have no rhyme or reason." When she indicated the desired facilities, he gave her a thankful look and hurried inside. "Just a moment, please."

Clayton found a stall and undid his pants. As he sat on the John, he reached under his fake skin, found the button, and tapped out a quick message. He waited thirty seconds, then heard an almost sub-sonic beep in his ear.

Knowing they'd gotten the message, Clayton stood and straightened his clothes. He flushed and exited the stall. After washing his hands, he patted a little at his cheeks, making himself appear flushed. Then he exited the room.

"Thank you," Clayton told her.

"Of course," Lorian replied with a smile. "Back this way a bit."

Considering her friendly attitude and obvious passion for her work, Clayton hoped that she wasn't involved with the shifter-human experiment end of it.

They retraced their steps a short ways, then took a different branch of the hall. Clayton was normally pretty good at direction, and he hoped that skill didn't fail him. According to the standard procedures that they'd gleaned for animal deliveries — thanks to a hefty bribe to a guard — Clayton had a pretty good idea of where Bailey would be taken. He just wasn't totally certain how fast he could get there.

The place had so many damn hallways.

Do they make it a maze on purpose?

Lorian stopped at a door in the hallway that looked like all the others. After knocking twice, she entered. "Hello, Doctor Nerian." She stepped backward and indicated Clayton. "May I introduce Doctor Ivan Kuzmich."

"Ah, Doctor Kuzmich," Doctor Nerian greeted, stepping forward with his hand outstretched while Lorian left, closing the door behind her. "It's so very good to meet you in person."

"The pleasure is with me," Clayton replied, shaking the man's hand. "I look forward to the exchange of ideas."

Releasing his hand, Nerian nodded. "And, of course, to the completion of both our works."

"Indeed. I have some ideas about that."

In truth, they were Drake and Edwin's ideas, and he really didn't want to share them, but he had to make it seem as if he were eager to get to work.

Nerian waved his hand negligently. "In due time, my new friend," he stated with a smile. "First, let us share a drink. There's a colleague who insisted on meeting you after reading your dossier and realizing what kind of shifter we would be working with."

Ah, so all pretenses are being dropped.

Still, Clayton arched one brow as if confused . . . or wary.

With an indulgent look on his face, Nerian crossed to the sideboard, raised a lid, and revealed a bar. "Oh, don't give me that look." He pulled out a bottle of vodka and three glasses. "We've seen each other's formulas. We know what we're working with."

Clayton cleared his throat, then forced a tight smile. "Forgive me for my reticence. Those in my country have had many . . . setbacks by trusting the wrong people."

Nerian nodded sagely as he poured their drinks. "I understand. So have we." With a dramatic sigh, he picked up two of the tumblers. "There are always those who are averse to progress."

"Indeed there are." The words tasted like ash in his mouth.

Lifting his glass, Nerian stated, "To scientists from two countries coming together to unravel a great mystery."

Clayton clinked his glass to Nerian's, then brought it to his lips. As he watched Nerian take a sip, he pretended to do the same. Then he lowered his glass and licked his top lip, sampling it.

Since it was a decent brand, Clayton said so.

Nerian grinned. "Glad you like it." A beep sounded at his desk, and he crossed to it. Pressing an intercom button, he asked, "Yes?"

"Doctor Winoan is here to see you, sir." Lorian's voice

came through the line.

Clayton felt his blood ice over in his veins.

Oh, fuck a duck.

"Excellent. Send him in," Nerian ordered.

Narrowing his eyes, Clayton demanded, "Who is that? I did not agree to speak with any other doctors."

Nerian lifted his hands in placation. "I know, but this man is brilliant. Trust me. Between the three of us" — he chuckled roughly — "well, the sky's the limit."

Smoothing his features into an impassive expression, Clayton responded non-committedly, "We shall see."

"Please, give him a chance," Nerian urged, and that was when Clayton saw it.

Nerian feared Winoan.

Not good.

Clayton dipped his chin in a tiny nod, then took an actual sip of his vodka.

When Nerian opened his door and welcomed Winoan, the man wasn't what he expected. The guy was a short, squat fellow who appeared to be of Japanese descent. He had a round face, glasses, and brown hair and eyes. There was nothing outstanding about the man at all.

Why is he — oh.

Winoan wasn't alone. Four men strode in after him. They were well-muscled with strong builds, and they moved with a grace that screamed military . . . or shifter.

Spotting a scar creasing the blond's left eyebrow, Clayton feared his heart had skipped a beat. *Miles Philson.* He glanced over the other three again, and a horrible realization struck.

These are Bailey's men.

Except, they were obviously acting as Winoan's bodyguards.

Don't panic.

Even as Clayton's mind whirled, he did what he did best. He worked under pressure. After all, being a bomb maker wasn't for the faint of heart.

With simple breathing focus, Clayton kept his pulse even. He ignored the four imposing warriors, hating how they looked at everything with a vacantness in their eyes and expressions. Even as Clayton feared that Winoan had managed to finish his project with Bailey's men, he wasn't going to figure it out by being discovered.

Eyeing Winoan, Clayton waited to be introduced. It took a moment since Nerian was busy verbally prostrating himself before the other scientist. Clayton felt a niggle of embarrassment on the other man's behalf.

Good grief.

Nerian finally seemed to gather enough self-control to remember they weren't alone in the room—maybe having guards was a normal thing. If that was the case, did Winoan have others under his control?

Only one way to find out.

When Nerian introduced Doctor Winoan, Clayton dutifully shook the man's hand, finding it a little cold and clammy. *Gross.* He barely resisted wiping his palm on his pants upon releasing him.

"So, you have brought a new project," Winoan said, jumping right in.

Clayton lifted his chin a smidge, silently displaying his displeasure as he replied, "It seems Doctor Nerian has been sharing my work with you."

Winoan chuckled nasally. "Only because he knew his mind could not do your work justice." He accepted the third glass of vodka from Nerian, not even bothering to thank the man. Instead, he remained focused on Clayton as he took a sip. Once Winoan had swallowed, he grinned broadly at him. "I am very looking forward to sharing thoughts with you on some of my own projects."

Never going to happen.

"I'm always happy to look over another's notes . . . when I

have time."

Winoan tipped his head back and laughed, the sound one similar to that of a braying donkey.

Yeah. A winner with the ladies, this one.

Before Winoan had even shut up, a low alert-style alarm sounded through the room.

Clayton knew exactly what was happening. Declan and his men were infiltrating the facility. Still, he couldn't allude to that.

After all, I'm a distraction . . . and I need to find Bailey.

After allowing his body to freeze for an instant first, Clayton sprung into action. "What have you done?" he screamed at Nerian. "You have compromised my life's work. Where is my cat? My work is nothing without him!"

"No, no!" Nerian lifted his hands in placation. "I promise, there must be some mistake. The alarm probably means nothing more than a mild toxin breach in the lab."

"I do not care what the alarm means," Clayton snapped. He threw his vodka glass at the wall, emphasizing his point. "You will take me to my cat . . . now! I will see for myself that he is well."

The breaking of the glass must have registered with the silent team, for they began to move forward as one, heading toward Nerian and Clayton as if to restrain them.

Winoan lifted a hand. "Halt."

They stopped.

Clayton narrowed his gaze, refusing to back down.

Dipping his chin in a slight nod, Winoan turned to Nerian. "Take us to Doctor Kuzmich's cat."

Nerian nodded swiftly. "Of course." He led the way out of the room.

His back straight and his strides sure, Clayton swiftly followed him. He swept his gaze left and right, barely moving his head. His whole façade was of confident arrogance, and he did everything to maintain it.

They'd passed a number of people trotting through hallways. There was an almost even mixture of guards and scientists. Their reports hadn't indicated nearly that many people on the ground.

Crapballs.

Knowing it wasn't his problem, Clayton focused on getting to his mate. He hated how close behind Winoan and his nearly silent sentinels were. His brain whirred with ideas on how to free Bailey's men from the scientist's influence.

Clayton followed Nerian into an industrial-sized space full of cages on rollers. All the beasts were sedated. Some of them were hooked up to IVs.

Goddamn. What is going on here?

He was almost afraid to discover the answer.

After winding through far more cages than Lorian had indicated *projects*, Clayton spotted a still sleeping Bailey.

Time to wake him up.

Moving to the corner of the cage, Clayton tilted this way and that. He pretended to be trying to see his mate's head, which was turned in the opposite direction. At the same time, he used his movements to hide what he was truly doing.

Ever-so-discreetly, Clayton pulled his tranquilizer gun from his pocket and loaded the special serum into the chamber. Unfortunately, when he fired it, the gun's soft *thwack* noise gave it away.

"Hey, what are you doing?" Winoan cried.

Clayton knew Bailey was already awake, but he was staying still to get the lay of the land. Spinning around, he pointed his tranq gun at Winoan. There were still two darts left — regular ones — so he had to be careful.

Sneering, Clayton stated, "I know what this invitation was all about. You can't fool me." He leveled the gun at Winoan, ignoring the way the soldiers began easing toward him. "You want to steal my research. Well, it's not happening. I'd rather it be dead than you take my life's work."

"Wait, wait." Nerian lifted his hands in placation. "That's not what's going on here at all." He appeared confused and troubled, clearly not understanding what was going on. "I really did just ask you here to collaborate."

Clayton spotted Bailey's ear twitch, and he smirked. "I know, Nerian. You're just another government stooge." Unable to help himself, he lifted his hand and fired his weapon at Winoan. "You, on the other hand, are a complete and utter waste of human space."

Winoan's wide eyes and gaping expression were so damn satisfying.

Unfortunately, considering it was a dart to sedate the man, he had time to point and say, "Kill him."

Bailey's former teammates started toward him, their eyes still just as blank and expressionless.

Clayton ripped open his jacket and yanked his pistol free of his fake flesh. He'd just steadied his weapon when a low warning yowl sounded at his back. He could feel Bailey's breath on his neck, and he froze.

Shit. Is he choosing them after all? No, not possible. That's not how mates work.

To his shock, Clayton wasn't the only one who froze. The four soldiers did, too. They appeared stiff and uncertain, as if they struggled with themselves.

Bailey licked the side of Clayton's neck once in reassurance. Then he yowled again, the sound still one of warning. There was also an undertone of anger in there, too.

His ex-team backed up a step, while glancing between each other. Then the black-haired man tipped his head to the side, and a strange questioning rumble came from his throat. The sound had a distinctive feline quality to it, even though it came from a human throat.

Bailey chuffed once, and all four men tipped their heads to the side in acceptance.

If Clayton hadn't seen it with his own eyes, he wasn't certain he would have believed it. Still, that didn't mean they were done. He trained his weapon on Nerian.

"Open the cage."

Nerian opened his mouth, then closed it again. The fear in his eyes intensified, but he did as he was told. He opened the cage.

Clayton rewarded him by shooting him with the second tranquilizer dart.

EPILOGUE

"I knew you weren't dead, Jared," stated a man who'd been introduced as Agent Craigson.

Bailey watched Prier shrug and smirk. "Don't let it get around that I'm helping the CIA now," the human teased.

Scoffing, Craigson rolled his eyes. "Oh, we wouldn't want to damage your reputation, would we?"

"What reputation?" Prier asked. "I'm dead, remember?"

"Of course, you are." Craigson turned his attention to Alpha Declan. "Thank you for clueing us in this time."

Alpha Declan dipped his chin in a nod. "It's time for us to work together."

Craigson nodded. "Agreed."

Then the agent eyed Bailey's former team members. The four men didn't seem to be able to acknowledge anything going on around them. They focused on the ground while watching Bailey in their peripheral vision.

"So, what about these guys?" Agent Craigson asked.

"They're coming with me," Bailey stated firmly, stepping forward even as he kept his arm firmly around Clayton. He wasn't going to allow his mate out of his sight for a long damn time. While Bailey wore only sweats, a t-shirt, and sneakers, he refused to allow that to daunt him, staring down the suit-clad man. "These are *my* men."

While Craigson didn't appear convinced, he nodded slowly. "Okay." He turned back to Alpha Declan and told him, "It's a pity we didn't get Doctor Nerian, but we'll catch up with him. Don't you worry."

Alpha Declan dipped his chin in a nod. "Thank ye."

Craigson eyed the alpha for a few more seconds, his eyes narrowing. The agent probably had his suspicions, but he didn't say anything. Instead, he turned on his heel and headed toward a nearby group of agents.

Declan turned and faced Clayton and Bailey, his lips twitching. In truth, Bailey had ordered two of his men to carry Winoan and Nerian out of the building. They'd been deposited into one of Declan's vehicles and whisked from the scene before any of the CIA could be the wiser.

"How are ye getting them to obey?" Declan asked curiously as he stepped close.

Bailey sighed deeply as he stared at the men he'd spent the last decade with. "Winoan gave us all cheetahs," he explained. "And I was the team leader. All their cats recognize me as their alpha."

Scoffing softly, Alpha Declan grinned. "Well, that's interesting." He sobered and promised, "We'll do everything we can to restore them, Bailey. Ye have my word."

Nodding, Bailey murmured his thanks.

Declan squeezed his shoulder lightly. "Order them into the SUV. Let's get out of here."

Bailey obeyed, shifting his throat to issue a soft commanding rumble. The cats within his four friends forced them to do as he wished, and they trooped into the SUV. As Bailey followed them, cuddling Clayton beside him on the bench seat, he wondered if anything could be done for his friends' minds.

As the vehicle started moving—their destination pack lands in Colorado—Bailey nuzzled his mate's neck, taking in his soothing scent, helping him to calm down. He knew it wasn't over, but it was a step in the right direction. For now, his mate was safe. His family was, too, and he'd found his team.

Cradling Clayton's chin, Bailey peered into his human's

eyes. "Thank you for staying safe. You are a true marvel."

When Clayton grinned back at him, Bailey dipped his head to taste those lips.

Just before he sealed his mouth over Clayton's, a thought flitted in and out of his mind.

Huh. Ronan said vampires can manipulate minds. I wonder if they can help.

Then Clayton's lips softened beneath Bailey's own, and all thoughts fled in the wake of his mate's taste.

YOU MAY ALSO ENJOY THE FOLLOWING FROM EXTASY BOOKS INC:

Playing With a Lawyer
Charlie Richards

Excerpt

Almost an hour later, Jory obeyed his vehicle's GPS prompt and turned onto a smoothly graveled driveway lined with fencing. He swept his gaze over the meadows broken by a smattering of trees here and there. Some of the cows seemed to be taking advantage of the shade, dozing beneath the bows.

As Jory drove by a few of the animals that were grazing close to the fence, he marveled at the idea that Attain had been herding the animals that afternoon. While he probably wouldn't admit it to anyone, he felt a little intimidated by the large beasts. Having grown up in the city, he hadn't been around live animals much.

His family hadn't even had a dog. His mother had been allergic. Instead, their family had had a large, saltwater aquarium in the parlor, but it had been a show piece, so guests could see his father's wealth.

Parking in front of a large ranch house, Jory shut off the engine. He hesitated, suddenly wondering if Ssimeas had the authority to invite guests.

Does Nicholas know I'm coming? Does Attain? Guess I should have worried about that before now.

Grabbing his phone, Jory intended to call Attain's line again. Before he could even wake his phone, the front door of the home opened and several men exited. He recognized Attain immediately, although he'd never seen him in jeans, a flannel shirt, and cowboy boots. Between that and the huge grin on his face, Jory decided Attain's lifestyle change looked good on him.

Jory recognized Nicholas Lindson, the owner of the ranch, from the news. There'd been a scandal involving his family. Evidently, the man Nicholas knew as his father — Baltus — was actually his uncle. Baltus's younger brother, Albert, was. That came out after Albert returned to the ranch with a male lover in tow, setting off the vengeful wrath of Nicholas's mother, Katrina.

There's probably more to that story, but it's not my place to ask.

As Jory eased from his vehicle, he took in the two men standing with Attain and Nicholas. They were, in a word, huge. The older-looking man with long, steel-gray hair who had his arm slung around Nicholas's shoulders had to stand over six and a half feet. The grinning, dark-featured male holding Attain's hip possessively was only a couple of inches shorter.

Jory had never considered his six-foot-one-inch frame small, but next to those guys . . . he did. Working out regularly, he kept himself in shape, but the men here were built like linebackers. He wondered briefly at the size of the horses they must need to carry someone their size.

Bet they have to ride draft horses.

Doing his best to hide his intimidation, Jory pasted on a smile and started toward the porch steps.

Attain greeted him with a smile. "Hey, Jory. It's good to see you again." He held out his hand, and the pair shook. Chuckling, Attain added, "I know you joining us has to be partly related to something from the firm, but Ssimeas coulda knocked me over with a feather when he told me you were coming."

Jory winced as he nodded. "Sorry. I hope it's okay."

"Of course, it's okay," Attain immediately replied. He waved toward Nicholas. "This is Nicholas Lindson, but you probably already knew that."

Nodding, Jory shook hands with the ranch owner. "I did, but it's nice to officially meet you." After releasing the man's work-roughened hand, he waved to indicate the area. "Your ranch is stunning."

"Good to meet you, too," Nicholas replied. With a wide smile, he swept his gaze over his spread. "Thanks. We surely do like it out here."

"I don't blame you," Jory replied. After a second, he added, "Thank you for letting me crash your barbeque."

"The more the merrier," Nicholas replied. Then he indicated the man next to him. "This is my fiancé Bodb."

Jory offered his hand. "Nice to meet you."

As the huge guy offered, "Same to you," and reached for his hand, Jory wondered if he would squeeze too tight in some kind of pissing contest. To his pleasant surprise, he didn't. His small smile appeared genuine, the corners of his eyes crinkling.

After letting go of Bodb's hand, the other big man held out his. "And I'm Ssimeas." With a wink, he added, "But you probably knew that already."

"I kinda figured," Jory replied with a grin. "What with you having that possessive hand on Attain's hip and all."

Ssimeas laughed heartily. "Guilty as charged. Can't help how much I love holdin' my man here." Then he leaned down and pressed his lips to Attain's.

Jory had never seen two men make out, and he felt an odd flutter in his gut. Even his groin warmed a little at the fierce display of propriety.

Nicholas chuckled as he patted Jory on his shoulder.

"Come on, Jory," he urged. "I'll show you around back while Ssimeas finishes ravishing Attain."

Jory nodded and followed, striding along the porch decking beside the other man.

"You'll have to forgive Ssimeas," Bodb added from Nicholas's other side. "He hasn't seen Attain much this afternoon, so he's feeling a need to reconnect with his lover."

"Sure, sure," Jory immediately replied. "I'd never tell another how to behave toward their significant other in their own home."

Bodb nodded as he peered over Nicholas's head at him. "Just wanted to be sure we weren't making you uncomfortable."

Jory shook his head, fighting the heat threatening his cheeks as he admitted, "Not that kind of uncomfortable."

"Aahhhh," Bodb murmured.

Nicholas clapped him on the back once, saying, "Well, come on around back. You'll have plenty of eye-candy here, and no one will be offended if you stare." With a wink, he continued, "Just no touching without permission."

"Uh, n-no, of course not," Jory stuttered, embarrassed as hell at the implications of their words.

Before Jory could say more, they rounded the last corner of the house and a sprawling, two-tiered deck stretched out before him. Many more men, and even a few women, milled around the space, and the fragrant scent of grilling meat perfumed the air. Jory's stomach rumbled.

With a smile, Nicholas guided him toward a group of people, and another round of introductions ensued.

ABOUT THE AUTHOR

Charlie started writing fantasy when she was eight, and after stumbling onto her first erotic romance at age nineteen, she realized her true calling. She now focuses on writing gay erotic romance, normally of the paranormal variety, with heroes of all kinds. With the help and support of her husband, Charlie finally fulfilled one of her life-long goals . . . move to acreage with her horses. You can often find her curled up with her laptop and a cup of tea or glass of wine, creating her next adventure. Charlie enjoys exploring the mountains of her new Oregon home on horseback, 4-wheeler, or motorcycle.

She can be reached at ch.richards2010@yahoo.com
Or visit her at www.charlie-richards.com